Kay's v[...]
became cold

"A man who kisses one girl while engaged to another is not to be trusted. In fact—he's despicable."

Rolf's eyes became chips of blue glass. "Why don't you seek proof before you condemn?" He paused. "Do you always get uptight when kissed by a man?"

"I am not uptight!" she snapped indignantly.

"No? You could have fooled me. Perhaps you're not kissed often enough. Have you a boyfriend?"

"That's none of your business," Kay retorted furiously.

"Which means the answer is no. It's surprising. You should be fending boyfriends off right and left."

"I've no wish to be fending them off. When I find the man I love, he'll be all I need."

He asked softly, "Then—you haven't found him yet?"

Miriam MacGregor began writing under the tutelage of a renowned military historian, and produced articles, books—fiction and nonfiction—concerning New Zealand's pioneer days, as well as plays for a local drama club. In 1984 she received an award for her contribution to New Zealand's literary field. She now writes romance novels exclusively and derives great pleasure from offering readers escape from everyday life. She and her husband live on a sheep-and-cattle station near the small town of Waipawa.

Books by Miriam MacGregor

HARLEQUIN ROMANCE
2710—BOSS OF BRIGHTLANDS
2733—SPRING AT SEVENOAKS
2794—CALL OF THE MOUNTAIN
2823—WINTER AT WHITECLIFFS
2849—STAIRWAY TO DESTINY
2890—AUTUMN AT AUBREY'S
2931—RIDER OF THE HILLS
2996—LORD OF THE LODGE
3022—RIDDELL OF RIVERMOON

Man of
the House
Miriam MacGregor

Harlequin Books

TORONTO • NEW YORK • LONDON
AMSTERDAM • PARIS • SYDNEY • HAMBURG
STOCKHOLM • ATHENS • TOKYO • MILAN

Original hardcover edition published in 1989
by Mills & Boon Limited

ISBN 0-373-03060-6

Harlequin Romance first edition June 1990

CHAPTER ONE

KAY blamed the gannets for the mishap. It had been their fault entirely, she decided. The large seabirds diving into the ocean off Napier Parade had distracted her attention, which was something the angry man should have been able to understand.

Had they also caught his notice and distracted his attention? Was that why he had been driving too close behind her? Of course that was it, and he had had the temerity to blame her. The tall handsome hulk—did being easy on the eye make him imagine he was also infallible?

It had been late in the afternoon and it had all happened so quickly. She had left several small paintings in one of the city's gift shops, and had turned on to the Marine Parade which would take her towards Te Awanga.

She had passed the paved area of the colonnade and the sound shell, where children were twisting and whirling along on narrow skateboards, and from the corner of her eye she had noticed numerous people moving about the greens of the little golf course. Then, while passing the lower level of the colourful sunken garden, she had seen the gannets.

Kay did not normally allow her attention to wander while driving the car, but the sight of the large white birds so near to the shore proved to be too much. She had been longing for a closer view of their plummeting into the sea, and there they were, wheeling against the azure of the January sky, the spread of their black-tipped wings catching the warmth of the New Zealand summer sun. Golden heads lowered, their sharp, searching eyes had caught the flash of a shoal of herring or mackerel in the blue waters below, causing sudden swift dives to snap at their prey.

A surge of excitement gripped her. Here was the action she longed to capture on canvas, but those rapid drops, straight as a ruled line, were always too distant for her to observe the exact positions of heads and wings during descent. And even if she *knew* they went down with wings at first half open and then wrapped close to the body just before the moment of impact, it wasn't the same as being able to *see*.

Never had she been quite so close to them, and she wondered if she could be quick enough to catch them on film. Fortunately her camera happened to be lying on the seat beside her, but would she be successful without a telephoto lens?

Such a luxury could be purchased only when better finances allowed, but that situation would not happen before Ivy was not so reliant upon Kay for company, and she would then be able to seek a job in Napier. After all, Ivy would not remain in a state of grief for ever.

In the meantime, and before she was earning a regular salary, she would have to rely on her own efforts and upon the quarterly cheque that came from the trust set up by her grandmother. It was not large, but it secured her from feeling penniless, and it at least helped to pay for art materials, which seemed to become more expensive every day.

As these thoughts flitted through her mind, an unexpected space in the long line of parked cars caused her to brake suddenly. It was beside the skating-rink, and as she nosed the yellow Mini into the kerbside she felt the small vehicle nudged by a definite bump from the rear.

A hasty glance over her shoulder showed that her sudden decision to stop had caused a red Porsche travelling directly behind her to swerve abruptly, but not before it had made contact with the back of the Mini.

And as the car passed she caught a glimpse of black-browed anger on the face of the man behind the wheel.

However, the Porsche did not stop, possibly because of its own following stream of traffic, and after waiting for a few moments Kay got out and went behind to examine the rear of the Mini. There was little to show that contact had been made with another car—apart from a smear of red paint on the bumper.

She then tried to assure herself that the Porsche would have suffered little damage because of her impulsive desire to brake, although a strong sense of guilt began to niggle at her as she snatched her camera from the front seat. Nor did it seem as if there was anything she could do about it, therefore she locked the Mini and hurried along the path between the skating-rink and the end of the sunken garden.

Moments later, she stood on the concrete path above the sloping shore which, instead of the sand usually found on New Zealand beaches, consisted of shingle brought down by the Hawke's Bay rivers. People lay on brightly coloured towels, sunbathing in the late afternoon heat, but Kay's interest was centred only upon the gannets still hurling themselves into the water.

She stood still, a slim figure with the sun glinting on her dark auburn hair. And as she squinted through the viewfinder, endeavouring to get a bird into focus, her concentration was so intense, she failed to notice the tall dark-haired man who stood watching her.

He had emerged from the path she herself had just followed, and when he spoke his voice rasped with anger. 'You're the driver of that yellow Mini.' It was an accusation rather than a question.

She lowered the camera, then turned to stare into a pair of blue eyes that glittered with a cold brilliance as they surveyed the cameo perfection of her face.

Guilt kept her silent.

'Don't try to deny it,' he snapped as she was about to

speak. 'I can recognise you. I saw your face, and those bare shoulders.' His dark brows drew together as he scowled, 'Do you always stop so abruptly in a stream of traffic and without a signal of any sort? I presume you're aware that you caused me to hit your bumper?'

She licked dry lips. 'You—you were in that red car?'

'Yes. It's the one now wearing a nasty paint graze on its left front wing. It doesn't suit it at all.'

'Then you must have been travelling too close behind me,' she flared defensively. 'There's a correct distance you should have been keeping.' There now, that would tell him she *did* know the rules of the road, even if she didn't always keep to them.

Blue ice glinted beneath the brows. 'If I'd been travelling too close the damage would have been worse, something like a dirty big dent. You women drivers must learn to signal your intentions to stop when the impulse to do so grabs you.'

She knew he was right about her failure to signal, and a faint flush touched her cheeks as she observed his hard jaw and his mobile sensuous mouth that was now set in a grim line. His expression caused her to say, 'I'm surprised you hadn't passed me earlier. People driving Porsches usually whizz past with a hiss and a roar.'

'That would have been pointless,' he snapped. 'No doubt it suits you to forget there was a line of traffic ahead, and that we were within the city speed limits.'

This, she realised, was a fact. The traffic was moving steadily on both sides of the tall, stately Norfolk pines that centred the Marine Parade entrance to Napier, and at last she said, 'Well, I can only say I'm sorry it happened, and I'll pay to have a paint retouch.'

'There's no need for that,' he said coldly, 'but I thought you should at least be aware of what you'd done. Perhaps it'll help you to remember to signal in future. Really, you women drivers are all the same.'

She became exasperated. 'I've said I'm sorry, and

perhaps I should explain that there was a reason for my sudden stop. You see, the gannets were diving and the parking-space loomed so unexpectedly.'

The dark brows drew together again. 'Diving gannets —parking-space. I suppose there's a connection somewhere.'

'I wanted to get a photo of them, but I'm afraid it's hopeless without a telephoto lens. Nor am I very good at photography.'

'Let me try.' He took the camera from her, then turned his attention towards the activities of the birds. A quick press of his finger and it was handed back to her with a brief comment. 'That might give you a dot against the blue. Perhaps it can be blown up into something more interesting.'

'Thank you. You're very kind to someone who has caused you trouble.'

He made no reply as his observation took in details of her soft brown eyes, her flawless complexion surrounded by the dark auburn shoulder-length hair with its slight wave that caused the ends to curl up. And from her face his gaze went to the sun-tanned shoulders, bare except for the narrow straps of her gold and brown check sundress.

As his scrutiny became more intense the pink in her cheeks deepened until, conscious of a rising embarrassment, she forced herself to say lightly, 'Would it be possible to see the damage I've caused?'

'Definitely. The car is in the parking-area.'

They walked beside the wall that sheltered the skating-rink from strong sea breezes, the path leading to a large area where rows of vehicles stood parked. Among them was the low-slung Porsche. As they drew near it she became filled with apprehension and was almost afraid to look at the car. Moments later she was appalled by the sight of the scratch marring the left front wing.

'That was done by the edge of your rear bumper,' he

told her. 'I doubt that it can be hidden by a smear of lipstick,' he added mockingly, his eyes on the curve of her sweet mouth which had become tremulous.

She gained control of herself. 'OK, so it is there, and no doubt it's most annoying to the car's proud owner. As I intimated before, I shall pay for the touch-up.' She snapped open her handbag, then wrote rapidly in a small notebook. Tearing out the page she handed it to him and said, 'There you are, that's my name and address. Please send the account to me.'

He studied the slip of paper in silence, his eyes becoming slightly narrowed.

She noticed his stillness. 'You can read it? Or do you consider my writing to be on a par with my driving?'

'Oh yes, I can decipher it. Kay Carlson, Hope House, Te Awanga. Spinster I presume?'

'Yes, if it's any business of yours.'

'And this Hope House?'

'I know it's an unusual name,' she cut in. 'It used to belong to a man named Arnold Hope, and I understand to his father before him. Please just send the account there.'

'You live there alone?'

'Certainly not. Mr Hope died and the place is now occupied by my mother's cousin, with whom I live.' She fell silent, annoyed with herself for having offered such information which could not possibly be of interest to this man.

But after all, what did it matter? If the account came she would pay it, and that would be that. She would never set eyes on him again which would be a pity, she reflected sadly, because she had met few men since coming to live with Ivy.

But at the moment she could find nothing further to say to this handsome sample of the male species, and, not wishing to appear anxious to begin a closer association, she said, 'Well, goodbye. I've still about thirteen miles to drive, and Ivy will be wondering where I am.'

'Ivy? She's your mother's cousin?'

'Yes. She's Mrs Wallace . . .' She fell silent before confiding that Ivy still hated to be alone in the house.

She left him abruptly, making her way back to the yellow Mini by walking along the Parade beneath the tall Norfolk pines. And as she unlocked the car she felt strangely different. It was almost as if she had had an adventure, and although she had met a man whose face seemed to do something to her, she also realised she didn't even know his name. So why this inner exhilaration?

Leaving the city of Napier, she continued to drive along the Parade between the pines that still flanked the highway, and at times her gaze strayed to follow the southern sweep of the bay which curved out to the gannet sanctuary on Cape Kidnappers. The seaside resorts of Haumoana, Te Awanga and Clifton were vaguely discernible before the long line of greyish-white cliffs led to the cape which, she had been told, was one of the few places in the world where the gannets nested on the mainland instead of on an island.

The road followed the coast, running past industrial areas and crossing three rivers before entering the township of Clive. It then turned left to run through flat, highly productive land where market gardens and vineyards flourished, and after crossing a fourth river it skirted Haumoana and went on to Te Awanga.

When Kay reached the waterfront house Ivy's smile betrayed her relief. 'It's lovely to see you come home, dear.'

'You've been lonely?'

'Yes. It's awful when the house is empty.'

'You should have come to Napier with me.'

'You're right, of course, but, well, I did some baking.'

'Arnold's favourite biscuits, I suppose.'

'You must admit they're nice.' She paused, then

uttered a sigh. 'I know I'm being stupid. I hate the house when it's empty, yet I hate leaving it.' Then, as Kay listened in silence, she went on, 'I suppose it's because I'm so used to having Arnold here—but I'll get over it, I promise you. I just need a little time.'

Kay's brown eyes reflected sympathy as they rested upon the older woman who was in her mid-fifties. At the same time she realised that Arnold Hope hadn't been here for six months, yet it seemed that Ivy was no nearer becoming accustomed to his absence. She was a small, slight person, and, looking at her critically, Kay said, 'I think you should eat more, Ivy. I've brought you some fillet steak.'

'That's very kind of you dear. I know there's not much of me. Arnold always declared that, small as I am, my heart is large. Now wasn't that sweet of him?' Her grey eyes misted at the memory of Arnold's words.

'And he was right,' Kay agreed, then, to avoid further reminiscences of Arnold's remarks she said, 'I remember that Mother had a favourite saying which concerned you.'

Ivy laughed. 'Oh, yes, your mother always maintained that although I wasn't very *strong,* I could certainly *cling.* Just like the ivy on the old garden wall,' she quoted.

Kay looked at her without speaking. Mother was right, she thought, because Ivy was still clinging to Arnold and to the house in which they had lived together.

'Well now, how did you get on in Napier?' Ivy asked. 'Did you find that one of your paintings had been sold in the gift shop?'

A smile spread over Kay's face. 'Yes, half a dozen fortunately, but just small ones. They were unframed and sold to tourists who can't be expected to carry anything that won't go in a suitcase.'

'Gannet paintings?'

'Three were of gannets, and I've been asked to do more. I'll have to get myself into gear, because now is the time when so many people go to see the gannet colony.' She stared through the window at the sparkling blue ocean. The sun had not yet descended behind the line of western mountain ranges and the sea appeared to be sprinkled with diamonds. Where was he now—that man?

Ivy said, 'You're a fortunate girl to have such a gift for painting. Yes, I know it's more than a gift, it's know-how and much observation. I wish I'd developed such a hobby. Now is the time when I need something to fill my mind.'

But Kay was hardly listening. Instead the blue of the ocean had reminded her of a pair of intensely blue eyes. Who was he? she wondered. No doubt he would be married. He looked as if he would be about thirty, or maybe just over, which would make him seven or eight years older than her own age of twenty-three. Yes, *of course* he would be married.

Her long silence caused a question to come from Ivy. 'You're very quiet. Is everything all right?'

Kay hesitated then said ruefully, 'Well, actually I had a bit of a mishap.' She explained how the paint on an expensive Porsche had become grazed.

'That sounds more like his fault than yours,' said Ivy thoughtfully. 'He must've been travelling too close behind you.'

'Yes, that's what I thought, but I've admitted I failed to signal. He was very angry, and I said I'd pay to have it fixed.'

Ivy brushed the incident aside. 'If I were you I'd forget about it. If he's a man who can afford to drive a Porsche he can afford to have the paintwork retouched. I doubt that you'll hear another word about it.' She moved from the lounge to the kitchen but paused in the doorway. 'Now then, you go to the studio and organise yourself for tomorrow's work, and I'll attend to the meal. Arnold always enjoyed fillet steak . . .'

Kay sighed. Arnold again. He was constantly at Ivy's side, she ·thought, as she went into the downstairs bedroom which had been converted into a studio for her. And now, as she looked unseeingly through the window, she recalled the day of her arrival six months ago.

It was after Arnold's death, and Kay had gone because Ivy had written a letter begging her to come and stay with her. At first Kay had hesitated, but her father had pointed out that she had just lost her job, while her mother had reminded her of the time Ivy had come at once when she herself had been laid low.

A few days later she had travelled from her home in Wellington to be met by Ivy at the coachline's Napier depot. Her suitcases and folding easel had filled the back of the yellow Mini and Ivy had then driven her to Te Awanga.

While driving along the Napier seafront road Ivy had thrown her an anxious glance. 'I hope the place won't be too dead for a girl of your age,' she had remarked almost apologetically. 'You'll find lots of houses there, but the population is divided between permanent residents searching for peace and quiet in their old age, and people who go there for holidays. It means that many of the houses are closed for most of the year.'

'Then I'll just have to keep myself busy,' Kay had replied, thinking of her art work. Be busy or be bored.

'Of course there are a few middle-aged people who live there because they like the place. I can only hope you'll like it too.'

Nevertheless, when they reached the seaside resort Kay had begun to wonder if she had made a mistake in leaving the bright lights of Wellington for this place of retirement, but she did not voice her doubts to her mother's cousin. She had made the decision to come, therefore she would stay for at least a short time. Since then the weeks had flown.

She recalled her first view of the house. 'It's larger than I expected,' she had exclaimed.

'Too large for only one person,' Ivy had said. 'But it's quite comfortable and sturdily built to withstand all the weathers that can sweep in from the South Pacific Ocean out there. It was built by Arnold's father, who had a farm inland but who loved to be near the sea.'

'So they came here for holidays?'

'Yes. As a boy Arnold spent many hours boating, swimming and fishing with his parents and sister Judith. Eventually his parents sold the farm and came to live here permanently, and by that time the place had become known as Hope House.'

'Where is Judith? Have you ever met her?'

'No. She's in Australia. She and her husband emigrated to Queensland about twelve years after their marriage, or maybe it was fifteen years. Now then, I'll make a cup of tea.'

As the days passed Kay had learnt more about Arnold. Apparently the time came when he decided to retire from his land development company and live at Hope House which he had inherited after the death of his parents. But the place did not suit his wife, who declared her brain to be too active for burial in a small area like Te Awanga.

According to Ivy she left him and went to live in Auckland with a man she had known for years, but the satisfaction she expected to find with this person was short-lived, because she died two years later. There had been no children of the marriage with Arnold, which had never been a happy one, and within a short time he was looking for a housekeeper.

'That's when he found me,' Ivy said, the memory bringing a rare smile of happiness. 'And my goodness, he certainly needed somebody to take care of him as well as the house, what with a lounge, kitchen, bedroom and lower bathroom downstairs, and three bedrooms and a bathroom upstairs the poor darling was just rattling round in the place.'

'You had ten years of happiness with him,' Kay said gently. 'You made everything right for him.'

Ivy nodded. 'Yes, I'm grateful for what we had, but now that he's gone the place is too big for me. I'm so thankful you agreed to come when I wrote.'

'Do you think you'll stay here—for ever?'

'It's what Arnold wanted me to do, and he made arrangements that enable me to do so. I'd be a mighty big fool not to comply with his wishes. His will left me the contents of the house, and gave me the right to live in it for the rest of my life, or until I wish to move out.'

'What about the expenses attached to the place?' Kay asked.

'The trustees pay the rates and any maintenance that's needed, which means I'm living rent free. Arnold also left me his shares, which give me a small income, so you see, although I never married him, he has taken care of me. Darling Arnold.' Her eyes misted, then filled with tears.

'Why didn't you marry him? You said he'd asked you.'

'Oh, yes, he asked me, but he also understood that I was afraid.'

Kay pondered Ivy's reply in silence because she did not understand, but at last she felt compelled to ask the question lurking in her mind. 'Why were you afraid? You loved and trusted him.'

Ivy hesitated. 'Well, you see, our relationship was so—so marvellous I didn't want to risk spoiling it. Arnold's marriage had been thoroughly unhappy, and mine had been disastrous, therefore we decided we didn't need any mumbled words or a signed slip of paper to prove we loved each other. Arnold needed me, and that was enough as far as I was concerned. Some people might say we were wrong, but we were happy with the arrangement.' She leaned forward to pat Kay's hand. 'You'll be tired of hearing me talk about Arnold, but it's so nice to have a listener.'

Kay smiled. 'Your invitation came just at the right moment for me.'

'Invitation! More of a plea, I think.'

'There's no fun in being made redundant. When I told the girls in the store I was coming to stay with you they were envious.'

'*Live*, dear, not stay.'

'Well—in the meantime,' Kay conceded, fighting off a sudden feeling of being trapped into a situation over which she had no control. Ivy's grief must not be allowed to rule her life for all time, she warned herself.

But it was really the unexpected that popped up to alter one's life, she mused, still reminiscing over those past days while searching through her gannet photos. Take the loss of her job, for instance. She had been working quite happily in the art department of a large Wellington store when the management had decided to do away with that section of the business. After the end of the month her services would be no longer required, she had been told.

A week later Ivy's letter had arrived. 'There's plenty for you to paint here,' she had written. 'I feel sure that souvenir paintings that are not too large would sell well in Napier. The place is full of tourists during the summer.'

Thinking it over, Kay had eventually heard the sound of a challenge. Could she earn enough from her own efforts with paint? And now she had to admit that the desire to try had been the real impetus behind her decision to join Ivy.

At first the results had been nil. The small paintings left in the Napier shops had remained unsold and Kay had begun to lose heart.

Ivy had become aware of her despondency and after one disappointing visit to Napier she had looked at Kay's downcast face and had said, 'Don't give up hope, dear. Let's go for a walk. You might see something that really inspires you.'

'Inspires me? Like what?'

'There might be an interesting bird on the roadside lagoon, so bring your sketch pad.'

'Perhaps you're right.' Kay knew that Ivy referred to an area of water lying between a stretch of waterfront road and the shingle-covered beach. It was surrounded by weeds and scrubby growth, although attempts had been made to beautify it by the addition of canna lilies, agapanthus and nasturtiums which gave colour during their flowering season.

'Who knows, it might be a turning-point,' Ivy had added.

And it had been. It was the period when October had slid into its third week, which meant that the entire country enjoyed the long weekend holiday for Labour Day. By Friday the cosy holiday homes nestling behind shrubs and trees had come to life, and there were caravans in the camping-ground.

It was the first time Kay had been in the wide grassy, tree-sheltered area with its buildings for toilets and showers, and its small shop for campers. They wandered along a path beside gnarled willows until it reached an opening which gave access to the shingle beach, and to a large fresh-water lagoon which offered safe splashing for children, although it was still too cold for swimming.

As they retraced their steps Ivy paused to lay a hand on Kay's arm. 'Look, there's a subject for you,' she whispered, indicating a man and his wife who relaxed in chairs beside their caravan.

The scene was not exactly inspiring, but Kay decided

to please Ivy by making the effort, therefore she approached the couple and said, 'Excuse me, would you mind if I sketch you?'

The woman smiled at her. 'Of course not, but you must promise to show us the result.'

'That won't be until tomorrow,' Kay explained. She then stood with her pad in hand and sketched rapidly, paying particular attention to the figures and details of the caravan. She indicated the trees and shaded the shadowed areas, at the same time pencilling in colour notes.

A man from a neighbouring caravan came to watch her work. 'Say, that's darned good. How about doing my van and the kids?' he asked. 'I'll pay you whatever you like to ask.'

'Tomorrow,' she smiled, suddenly feeling enthusiastic.

When she reached home she transferred the sketch to a rectangle of good quality watercolour paper that would not buckle when a wash was applied to it, then squeezed dabs of colour on to a palette. She washed in the sky, trees and foreground before attending to the more detailed aspects of the caravan and figures, and by the time she went to bed she had a small but presentable painting.

Ivy was amazed. 'You've almost finished it,' she exclaimed.

'Not quite. Tomorrow I shall take it out to the spot and complete the details. It won't matter if the shadows have changed because I've already put them in.'

The results of her work had been most satisfactory. The owners of the caravan were delighted to see such a souvenir of their camping weekend and promptly purchased the watercolour. And then the man in the neighbouring van dared his children to move while she sketched them.

By the time the camping-ground had become empty

late on Monday afternoon she had completed and sold
six small paintings. Her prices had been kept modest
because the works were unframed and without the glass
necessary for watercolours, although she had attached
each one to a mount which improved its appearance by
setting it off.

Monday night found her mentally exhausted by the
constant concentration, yet the busy weekend seemed to
herald a turning-point in her luck, because next time she
went to Napier she found she had sold another six
paintings.

In November Kay made a start on painting the
gannets, the work being done from photographs she had
taken after visits to the reserve. The large migratory
seabirds had come from eastern Australia, arriving in
late July to nest in many thousands of pairs.

She had been fascinated by their ritual breeding
displays of long necks and crossed beaks which made
interesting studies in oils and watercolours. During the
summer months they received much of her attention
because she knew that by April most of the birds would
have returned to Australia. And now she had been
asked for more paintings of them, therefore she would
begin a sketch immediately.

She dragged her easel nearer the window for better
light, then froze as a flash of red caught her attention. It
came from a car moving slowly along the road, the sight
of it causing her to catch her breath. Surely it was the
Porsche? Little observation was necessary to recognise
the low-slung sporting lines of the car, and her mental
vision saw the deep scratch marring the side of its left
wing.

Had he come searching for her, perhaps to acquaint
her with the estimated cost of the repair work? Hope
House was easy enough to find because the building was
not far from the road and a board on the wall gave the
place its name.

The car stopped at a house situated a short distance along the road, and Kay had no difficulty in recognising the tall man who got out. She watched him walk round to open the passenger door, and it was only then that she realised he was not alone. Nor was the girl who alighted a complete stranger to her.

Estelle Barron was a few years older than Kay, and as she watched the slim redhead accompany the car's owner into her mother's home Kay wondered just how friendly they were.

Was it her imagination that Estelle clasped his arm and laughed up into his face? Did he seem to bend towards her, or was it just a trick of the late afternoon light?

So what? Kay demanded of herself crossly. He was welcome to Estelle, just as she was welcome to him.

CHAPTER TWO

KAY recalled the day she had met Estelle Barron. It had been during a weekend when she had taken a walk to buy extra milk at the corner shop. The flash of sun on Estelle's brilliant red hair had caught her attention, and then the older girl's green eyes had stared into hers.

Estelle had been the first to speak. 'Aren't you the person living with Ivy Wallace?' she had demanded in cool tones.

'Yes, Kay Carlson.' She had introduced herself with a smile, feeling pleased to meet someone near her own age.

But Estelle had not exuded friendship. Instead she had adopted a superior air as she had said, 'I'm Estelle Barron. I live four doors along the road from you in that large place with the portico and pillars. You've probably heard of me.'

Kay was nonplussed. 'No, I'm afraid I haven't . . .'

'Surely Ivy Wallace has told you everything about everyone living along the seafront?'

Kay shook her head. 'Gossip is the least of Ivy's activities. She hasn't told me anything about anybody.' Apart from Arnold, Kay added silently to herself.

'Oh. Well, I have a boutique in Napier. Very exclusive. Estelle for Style, you know.'

'That's nice for you.' Kay's tone remained polite but vague.

'No doubt you've heard of my mother, Mrs Lexington-Barron,' Estelle persisted. 'She's on numerous committees, and she knows most of the important people in Napier. She likes to retain her maiden name,' she added as an afterthought.

Kay said nothing, having no wish to admit she had never heard of Mrs Lexington-Barron.

'Mother attends to many good works,' Estelle told her. 'I happen to know she's been wondering about Ivy Wallace. I mean, she's been wondering if she can *help* her.'

Kay was puzzled. 'I'm not aware that help is needed. In what way could your mother help Ivy?'

'Well, with her housing problem, of course.'

'*Housing* problem? She hasn't got one.'

'Of course she has. That house is too big for one person.'

'But I'm with her now.'

Estelle laughed. 'Te Awanga won't suit you for long. It's a backwater where nothing ever happens.'

'It might surprise you to learn it's suiting me very well. I've been kept busy from the moment I arrived.'

Estelle's eyes had widened. 'Busy? Doing what?'

'Small paintings that are sold to tourists.'

'Then of course you should be living nearer to the city. I'm sure Mother could help you both find a place, something small and cosy.' The smile that had broken over Estelle's face altered her entire expression. It showed even white teeth, a flash of dimples, and made Kay realise she was really quite beautiful.

But the smile vanished as quickly as it had come. 'How long does she intend to stay in that house?' The question held a ring of arrogance.

Kay was startled. 'How long? I really don't know.'

'She doesn't *own* it, you know.' The tone had now become waspish.

'I'm aware of that, but she has the right to live in it for the rest of her life.'

'Or until she decides to move out,' Estelle had snapped pointedly.

Kay had shaken her head. 'I don't think she's likely to do that.'

'What on earth keeps her at Te Awanga?' Estelle had exclaimed, her tone betraying impatience.

'Arnold's memory.' Kay stopped, annoyed with herself for having allowed the words to slip out.

'She must have had a mighty firm hold on him. Men can be so—so *gullible*.' The words dripped with acid.

Kay had left the shop seething with anger, and when she had reached home she told Ivy she had met the red-haired girl from along the road. However, she made no mention of their conversation.

And now it appeared that—*that man*—had driven Estelle home from her Napier boutique, and again Kay wondered about the closeness of the relationship between them. No doubt she had been shown the scratch on the expensive Porsche, and no doubt she had been told it had been done by someone from Te Awanga, someone living in Hope House.

Ivy entered the room to disturb her ponderings. 'What's happening out there, dear? You appear to be very engrossed.'

'Do you see that red car parked outside the Barrons' house? I don't suppose you know who owns it.'

Ivy moved to stand beside Kay at the window, then shook her head. 'No, but then I don't move within their circle of friends. It looks rather smart, and somewhat costly, I'd say.'

'The owner has just driven Estelle home.'

Ivy's lips twitched into a wry smile. 'I'm sure Mrs Lexington-Barron will approve of the transport. Did you happen to see the driver? I presume it's a man.'

'Oh, yes, I saw him, and I've seen the car before now. It's the one I damaged by stopping too suddenly.'

'You mean it's the one that was following too closely. I wish you'd stop worrying about it. If it's just a simple scrape he'll have it fixed in no time.'

But Kay's memory was not visualising the damage on the car. Instead she was looking into a pair of blue eyes that sparked with anger from beneath straight dark brows, and again she saw the hard jaw and tight line of his mouth.

Unexpectedly, she became conscious of a strange desire to see that same face when it held a different expression, one that was without anger towards her. But that was unlikely to occur because, even if they did happen to meet, his attitude towards her would be influenced by the thought of damage to his precious Porsche.

Nor was she able to push the vision of his face from her mind, and as she unwrapped several new tubes of oil paint, sharpened a few watercolour pencils and checked her outdoor sketching-satchel, his image seemed to hover about the room.

During the evening meal Ivy said, 'Have you decided upon tomorrow's work, dear?'

She pushed the handsome face away from her mind. 'Tomorrow? Oh yes, I thought I'd walk to the roadside lagoon. Weather permitting, of course. I've been hoping to see one of those lovely dark blue swamp hens with its red beak and legs.'

'You mean a pukeko. Let's look at the sky.' Ivy left the table and went to stare through the window at the end of the lounge. 'Ah, stratus clouds,' she exclaimed, gazing towards the distant ranges. 'Arnold always warned that those long horizontal streamers indicate wind. He said that Te Awanga is the Maori word for the south-west wind. Dear Arnold, he knew so much about these things,' she added with a small sigh.

'Then I'll have to search for a sheltered place,' Kay decided.

'If it's too windy you'd be wiser to work in the studio. You've plenty of photos to give you ideas.'

'Yes, but I prefer to work from the actual models whenever possible. Photos are really for winter work.'

Next day the weather proved that the stratus clouds

had not lied. The south-west wind swept across the plains from the mountains, and as Kay carried her satchel and folding stool along the road towards the roadside lagoon she knew she should have taken Ivy's advice by remaining in the studio.

However, she found a place where she could set her stool beside tall coastal-growing shrubbery which was dense with small shiny leaves that gave protection. It was also a place from where she had a view of the orange canna lilies and blue agapanthus which were now in full bloom.

Several wild duck were sheltering near reeds growing beside the banks, and as she sketched the shapes of heads and bodies a shadow fell across the pad resting upon her knee. Startled, she looked up to meet the intensely blue eyes of the owner of the red Porsche, the unexpectedness of his appearance leaving her speechless.

He had come upon her from the seaward side of the sheltering shrubbery, his pale fawn short-sleeved shirt unbuttoned to reveal a broad chest covered with crisp dark hairs, his matching shorts revealing well-formed legs. When he spoke his voice betrayed surprise. 'Hello, we meet again.'

'Hello.' The sepia watercolour pencil remained poised in her hand. She disliked being watched while she worked, nothing being more guaranteed to cause errors, but even as she waited for him to move on she realised he had no intention of doing so.

Instead an amused expression crossed his face as his deep voice drawled, 'Do you always choose a windy day for sketching? It seems rather odd to me.'

She forced a smile. 'But then you've already decided I'm idiotic.'

He frowned. 'Seriously, why come out on a day like this?'

'Because it gives me movement. You can see the bend

in the reed tops, the lean on the canna lilies above them, the ripples on the water. If I can capture that sense of movement the result will be given a little life. It will not be completely static.'

'Is this how you spend your days?'

'Yes.'

'I mean, you don't hold down a job of some sort?'

'No.'

'Are you saying you're a full-time artist?' he persisted.

'I'm *trying* to be one,' she admitted hesitantly, aware of his scrutiny that took in every detail of her appearance. Her silky green dress with its cap sleeves and softly flared skirt came in for his special attention, and she knew that his eyes rested upon the mounds below its low neckline.

'You don't look particularly poverty-stricken,' he remarked at last. 'At least, not the starving-in-a-garret type of artist.'

'I should hope not,' she declared indignantly. 'Nor do I look upon my studio as a garret. It's a very respectable downstairs bedroom, or it was until Ivy handed it over to me.'

'Oh, yes, Hope House, I think you said. I'd like to see your studio.'

'Oh? For what reason?'

'Because I'd like to see some of your work.'

'I can't imagine why you'd be interested in my work.'

'Is it not for sale? You have no completed paintings on hand?'

'Yes, but they're all small ones, suitable for tourists or people on holiday to carry in suitcases. If you're expecting to see large land or seascapes in ornate frames you'll be disappointed.'

'Then you will invite me into your studio?'

'Very well.' He might at least introduce himself, she thought, becoming vitally conscious of the bare legs with their dark hairs standing so close to her stool. He knew who *she* was, but she had no idea of *his* identity. Nor would she deign to ask his name. It was most irritating.

She closed her sketch-pad and began to replace the pencils in their flat tin box, each one being put in its correct colour position. 'Shall we go now? Hope House is just along the road.'

'I know exactly where it is,' he told her quietly.

'I suppose you noticed the name on the wall when you drove past last evening.' The remark just slipped out, then, annoyed with herself for having uttered it she hastened to explain, 'I happened to be at my studio window when I saw the flash of a red car.'

'And of course you recognised it, having met it earlier in the day. You can stop worrying about it,' he added. 'I've already made arrangements to have the damage repaired.'

He insisted upon carrying her stool and satchel along the road, and as they walked the wind blew Kay's dark auburn hair back from her face. It whipped colour into her cheeks. At least, she told herself it was the wind that made them feel flushed.

When they reached the house she turned to lead him into the short driveway, but found he had paused to stare at the building. 'It was built in the 1930s,' he remarked.

She was surprised. 'Yes, somewhere about then, I believe. How did you know?'

'Oh, there are several points that hit an architect's eye.'

'You're an architect in Napier?'

'Yes, I'm there now. I've been in Australia for years, but when this partnership in Napier was offered to me I decided to accept it.'

'How long have you been back in New Zealand?'

'For only a few months.'

'Oh.' She had learnt a little more about him, but still his name remained hidden within the depths of the unknown. Not that she cared whether it was Tom, Dick or Harry, of course.

He remained immobile apart from his head, which turned to examine the narrow stretch of lawn fronting the house, the profusion of pink and red flowers on the hibiscus shrubs, and the petunias bordering the drive. There were geraniums wherever Ivy had been able to poke cuttings into the soil, but it was the flowering gums that really caught and held his attention.

Tall, gnarled, and massed with orange-red blooms, their flamboyant beauty held his gaze for several long moments before he said, 'Who attends to the garden?'

'Ivy and I do it together.' Kay was surprised by his interest in the care of their grounds which, though small, were well laid out and colourful. Nor did she feel inclined to explain that as far as Ivy was concerned it was still Arnold's garden, and to be kept as a shrine to his memory.

She led him towards the back door which was situated beneath the shelter of a carport. The absence of the Mini indicated that Ivy had gone out, and as she took the door key from its place of concealment she said, 'Ivy's probably gone to the corner shop for a few groceries. I'm sure she'll be home soon.'

A mocking glint sparked in the blue eyes. 'Are you saying you'd rather I didn't come in, that you'd prefer I waited for Ivy's return?'

'No—no, of course not.' The words were hesitant.

'I assure you, there's no need to be afraid of me.' The mocking glint was still there, and with it a twisted grin.

He was perceptive, she realised, knowing that she *had* felt a sudden apprehension about inviting this stranger into the house. But it vanished abruptly, enabling her to say in a calm manner, 'What makes you imagine I'm afraid of you? It's just that I'd like Ivy to—to meet the man whose precious possession I've ruined.'

'Precious possession, *ruined*? You've got to be joking. Now where are these paintings?'

She felt a sudden reluctance to display her work. 'You'll probably consider them to be juvenile daubs. It's possible your preference leans more towards abstract painting.'

'Why must you jump to these conclusions?'

Despite his request he did not appear to be in a hurry to view her work, because he lingered in the kitchen while sending an appraising eye over the cupboards, sink bench and electric stove. And in the lounge he paused to look about him before following her into the studio, which held a distinct odour of turpentine and linseed oil.

The divan bed, pushed against the wall and covered by an old bedspread, served as a wide bench to hold art materials. The dressing-table and tallboy had been put to similar use. A table near the window held a box of watercolours, while her easel displayed the early stages of an oil of two gannets, their strong beaks crossed and pointing skyward during a courting session.

However, the painting that caught his attention was a portrait in oils of Ivy. It was one of the few Kay had had framed, and it hung on the wall at the end of the room.

'This is the person with whom you live?' he asked.

'Yes, that's Ivy. She sat for me.'

'You do many portraits?'

'Only when someone will sit for me. I enjoy the challenge of portraiture. A scene can be manipulated for the sake of composition, but a portrait has to be correct. The eyes, nose and mouth must belong to the subject, otherwise the likeness is lost, therefore careful drawing is most necessary.'

He turned to look through a small pile of unframed watercolours lying on top of the tallboy, then paused when he came to a study of Hope House.

She had sketched it from across the road, and now she knew a moment of panic. He's an architect, he's sure to notice errors in the perspective, she thought, then waited for his criticism.

But it did not come. Almost as if reading her thoughts he turned to her with a grin. 'Your perspective's not bad—quite good, in fact. And I like your colours. They're strong without being garish. And they're clean. Watercolour should always be *clean*. You see, I'm not entirely ignorant about these matters.'

His praise generated a warm glow somewhere inside her while a flush crept into her cheeks. 'Thank you for the kind words.' Then she felt tempted to ask, 'How do you find my oils?'

His eyes rested upon them thoughtfully. 'There's a pleasing softness about them. They'd be easy to live with. However, I'd like to see you do larger paintings.'

She gave a faint smile. 'To be honest, I prefer to work on a larger scale, but I'm restricted by what will sell to people who must carry them in a suitcase.'

'Yes, I suppose so.' He returned to the pile of watercolours, turning each one over. 'I see you've put prices on the backs.'

'Yes. It was Ivy's idea. She said it would keep me from dithering over the question during a sale. People could see the price and they could take it or leave it.'

'A sensible person, by the sound of her.'

'Indeed she is. I'm sure you'll like Ivy.'

'Ah, but Ivy might not like me,' he murmured enigmatically.

The remark puzzled her, but before she could ask what gave him such an idea he said, 'I'll take this one.'

Her eyes widened. 'Hope House? Why would you wish to buy a painting of this place?'

'It's not for myself, it's for somebody else.' He drew a wallet from a buttoned shirt pocket and extracted several notes.

'Thank you.' Kay felt shaken. It was the quickest and most unexpected sale she had ever made. 'I'm sorry it's not framed.'

'I don't want it framed. I intend to post it.'

'Really?' She waited for further information but it did not come.

And then the sound of the returning Mini caught their ears. The kitchen was just through the wall from the studio and they heard Ivy enter the house. There was a faint sound of packages being dumped on the kitchen table before her voice called, 'I know you're home, dear. I *said* it would be too windy for sketching out of doors.'

Kay left the studio. 'We have a visitor, Ivy.'

The man followed her into the lounge, and as Ivy came from the kitchen the sight of him brought her to an abrupt halt. Her eyes widened and the colour left her face as her jaw sagged slightly. She then took a deep breath as though to gain control, and within moments had recovered her poise.

However, Ivy's consternation had not escaped Kay, and she was curious to know what had upset her. As soon as this man departed Kay would be ready with a string of questions, she decided, but in the meantime she made an attempt to introduce them by saying, 'This is Mrs Wallace, but I'm afraid I'm unable to tell her your name.'

He strode across the room to shake hands with Ivy. 'Rolf Warburton. We'd have met sooner or later, I think.'

'Rolf—Warburton?' Ivy echoed faintly, and again her eyes widened into twin grey pools.

Kay said, 'Mr Warburton has just bought one of my paintings, the watercolour of Hope House.'

'Really? Well, I'm not surprised.' Ivy's voice shook slightly.

'You're not? I'll admit his choice surprised me,' Kay

exclaimed. 'People don't usually buy paintings of houses unless they mean something to them.'

'Your watercolours are very nice,' said Ivy hastily.

Rolf Warburton spoke to Ivy, his voice serious. 'Now that I've met you I can see that her portrait work is also very good. In fact, I'm already considering a commission for her.'

Kay turned to look at him. 'Are you saying you wish to sit for me?'

He uttered a deep throaty laugh, and with it his face seemed to be transformed. 'Me? Oh, no, I'm afraid I'm too impatient to sit still for more than five minutes. The commission I had in mind concerns a friend. I'd like you to do a portrait of her.'

'Her?' Kay knew she should be delighted, but strangely she was conscious only of disappointment.

'Estelle Barron,' he went on. 'She lives a few doors along the road. I'm staying with them this weekend.' He turned to Ivy. 'I feel sure you've met Mrs Lexington Barron.'

Ivy's lips thinned. 'Not socially. Mrs Lexington Barron considers herself to be on an—an upper level, if you understand what I mean.'

Rolf frowned. 'Surely she speaks to you?'

'Oh, yes, she speaks if we happen to meet in the corner shop, but she does not invite a neighbour's *housekeeper* into her home. Oh no. And that's all I'll ever be to her, a neighbour's housekeeper.'

'And that worries you?' Rolf asked quietly.

'Not at all,' retorted Ivy. 'I was proud to be——' She lapsed into a sudden silence as though fearing she was about to say too much, then changing the subject abruptly she said, 'Would you like to stay and have lunch with us?'

He said, 'Thank you, that's very kind, but I'll be expected at the Barrons' table. I'm their guest.'

'Estelle will be wondering where you are,' Kay said, unable to resist the remark.

'That's possible.' His tone was serene. 'So what about the portrait? Will you agree to do one of her?'

Within the last few moments Estelle Barron had become the last person on earth Kay wished to paint, but she told herself to be reasonable. A portrait was always a challenge, she had told him earlier, and common sense now told her she would be stupid to turn down a commission. Heaven alone knew what it could lead to, perhaps other commissions if it turned out to be sufficiently successful.

'Well?' The word was snapped with impatience. 'Do I detect a reluctance on your part?'

'Of course she'll do it,' Ivy put in quickly.

'You might find difficulty in persuading Estelle to sit for me,' Kay warned. 'She might suspect I'm unable to do her—justice.'

'She'll sit,' he declared with confidence. 'Naturally, I'd like you to do her in oils, about the same size as the one on the wall.'

'Ivy's? It's done on a sixteen by twenty-inch canvas panel,' Kay told him.

'That'll do nicely.'

'Then you can tell her I'll need three sittings, each of two hours' duration.'

'You mean you'll expect her to sit perfectly still for two hours?'

'No. The time will be divided by rest periods, but the sittings must always be at the same time of the day so that the highlights and shadows are more or less in the same place.'

'Right. I'll tell her to get in touch and you can make arrangements. See if you can emphasise the sweeter side of her nature,' he added with a grin.

Ivy said shrewdly, 'I believe you're rather fond of this girl.'

He appeared to think about the question before he said, 'One usually becomes fond of old friends.'

'You've known her for a long time?' Ivy pursued.

'We played together as children. In those days I found myself in the role of guardian because she's a little younger than I am. It was my duty to see that she didn't go too far out when swimming, and if we were near the Kidnapper cliffs I had to be sure we weren't caught by the tide.'

'She always obeyed you?' Ivy's tone was dry.

'Indeed no. Estelle has a rashness that goes with red hair.'

Kay found herself beginning to enjoy this man's presence, and when she asked herself why this should be, the answer was plain enough. It was because she had had contact with him without knowing his identity. He had been a mystery man, and this had intrigued her.

Oh, yes, he was also a handsome male with an aura of magnetism oozing from every pore of his athletic body, but this had little to do with it. She had seen athletic bodies before now. There had been plenty of them standing as models in the life classes at art school, but she had never felt drawn towards them, had never felt the urge to know more about them.

So why was she now listening with avid interest to every word that offered further scraps of information about this man?

She became aware that he was leaving. Ivy was ushering him into the hall where he appeared to pause and gaze up the stairs, no doubt examining the wall panelling, banisters and stair handrail with the critical eye of an architect. Moments later she could see him striding along their short drive while Ivy stood like one in a trance, staring after his departing form.

Kay went to stand beside her. 'Do you realise he's the man whose car I damaged?'

But it was as if she hadn't spoken because Ivy ignored the question as she closed the door and leaned against it. Then her voice shook as she said, 'My dear, I think I'll have a sherry before lunch. I—I feel as if I need—something—to steady me.'

Kay became concerned. 'What's the matter?'

Ivy made no reply as she walked slowly towards the lounge where she sank into a chair.

Kay became even more concerned as she followed her into the room. 'Ivy, are you all right?'

'Yes—yes—just give me a sherry, a good one in a larger glass.'

Kay went to the cabinet and poured two drinks, and as she carried the brimming crystal glass across the room she watched Ivy narrowly. 'You can't fool me, Ivy,' she said. 'I know something is wrong. It's not my imagination that you're feeling somewhat shaken.'

'My dear, *he's so like Arnold*—it gave me quite a turn. Can't you see the likeness to that photo in my bedroom?'

'I really hadn't thought about it.'

'The build of him, that dark hair, those blue, blue eyes that can be so piercing. Oh, yes, he's exactly as Arnold would have been at his age. I can tell you, I've had a shock.'

Kay felt a surge of sympathy for Ivy. Just when she was settling down to life without Arnold his ghost appears, or someone very like it; and in an attempt to divert the older woman's mind she repeated her former remark by saying, 'When I introduced you I was longing to say that this is the person whose car I damaged.'

Ivy looked at her in silence, almost without comprehension.

'You remember, I told you about the Porsche. He said arrangements had been made to fix it.'

Ivy sipped her sherry, then gazed into space as she murmured, 'I'm afraid his car is the least of our worries.'

Kay became impatient. 'For Pete's sake, Ivy, what's the matter?'

Ivy turned to her, her grey eyes wide. 'Don't you realise who he is?'

'He said his name's Rolf Warburton. He's an architect.

He lived in Brisbane for years but now he's joined a firm in Napier. Further than that I know nothing.'

'Oh, but there's lots more. Arnold's sister married a Warburton and they went to live in Australia. They had one son, and *that man* is Arnold's nephew.'

Light dawned upon Kay. 'That's why he bought the painting of Hope House. Now I understand.'

'Exactly. A man could look like Arnold, but only a connection of his would want a painting of Hope House.'

'He said it was to be posted.'

'To his mother, no doubt. And let me tell you something else. He owns this place. Arnold left it to him.'

Kay's jaw sagged. '*Owns* it? But I thought you told me——'

'I told you that Arnold's will left me the *right to live in it* for my life, or until I decide to move out of it. And the moment I do, his nephew may take possession of it. When Arnold died the situation was different because his nephew was in Australia and unlikely to need the house, apart from money from its sale.'

Kay sat listening in silence, waiting to hear more of Ivy's fears.

'The solicitor told me that the owner of the house would not need to sell it because he'd been well provided for by grandparents on his father's side, and in any case he'd be sure to respect Arnold's wishes.' Ivy's face became pathetic as she turned to Kay. 'But now he's in Napier. He could possibly want to get married and live in it.'

'You mean to Estelle Barron?'

'I'd place her as a high contender for his affections. If he's like Arnold in character as well as in appearance.' She sighed, falling silent as her eyes filled with unshed tears, then she held her glass towards Kay. 'Fill it up again, I need another.'

Kay tried to sound practical. 'Lunch is what you need.' Nevertheless, she refilled Ivy's glass and her own.

Ivy continued to analyse the situation. 'He's staying with the Barrons for the weekend. Doesn't that tell you anything?'

Kay said nothing, fearing that it did.

'*And* he's arranged for her portrait to be painted. He wouldn't do that without a strong reason. I'm telling you, he's serious about Estelle Barron. He'll want us out of this house.' Her voice quavered as she uttered the last words.

Kay tried to comfort her. 'You're worrying needlessly, Ivy. You're forgetting Arnold's will concerning yourself. Why not put the whole issue out of your mind? Let's wait and see what happens.'

'How can I, with that girl coming to have her portrait painted?'

'It was you who assured him I'd do it,' Kay reminded her.

'I must have been completely daft. And now every minute of every sitting she'll be planning the alterations she'll make. I don't want to think of Arnold's house being changed,' she almost wailed.

Kay's tone became gentle. 'Ivy, love, you must remember that in this life nothing stays the same. We are all subject to alteration. Now then, I'll make you a salad with lettuce, tomato, jellied beetroot, cheese and all the things you like.'

'Thank you, Kay, I don't know what I'd do without you. And I certainly don't want to see you lose your studio. You know, this business could affect you as well as me.'

Kay pondered those words as she pulled lettuce apart and dunked it in cold water. She had no wish to lose her studio, nor, like Ivy, had she any wish to leave Hope House. How much confidence could they place in Arnold's will? Would it stand up in a court of law, or could it be contested?

During lunch Ivy continued to look thoroughly

downcast.

'Cheer up,' Kay said, noticing how little she ate.

'I can't cheer up. I feel miserable. Suppose people start pointing the bone at me? Suppose they suggest I should vacate the house so that the rightful owner can move in with his bride?'

'Then you must decide which is more important to you, public criticism or Arnold's wishes spoken loudly and clearly through his will. Personally I think you're crossing your bridges before they're even in sight.'

'Do you really think so?' asked Ivy anxiously.

'You haven't yet been asked to move?'

'No, not yet.'

'And Estelle Barron has not yet announced her engagement to Rolf?'

'No.'

'So that at present your fears are based on mere supposition.'

'Except that his wish for her portrait is something to wonder about,' Ivy reminded her drily.

'I suppose so.' The thought had also been simmering in Kay's mind, but she did not care to admit it. Nevertheless, when lunch was cleared away she spent time in the studio checking her art materials, making sure that her oil-box held tubes of burnt sienna, yellow ochre, vermilion, alizaron, cobalt blue, viridian and of course titanium white. At least she was prepared—that was, if the event came to pass.

By five o'clock that afternoon the wind had abated, and although Kay had spent most of the time in the studio she had been able to hear Ivy's movements in the kitchen. The constant opening and shutting of drawers indicated that a general clean-up was in progress, an occupation to which Ivy often turned when something had upset her, and the activity through the wall told Kay that the shock of meeting Rolf Warburton had gone deeper than she had realised.

Kay had been completing the scene she had begun at the roadside lagoon, but now she laid down her brush and went through the lounge and into the kitchen where she found Ivy replacing dishes in a cupboard. 'Let's go for a walk,' she suggested with forced brightness. 'I could do with a breath of fresh air.'

Ivy sent her a wan smile. 'Very well, dear. Perhaps it would do me good. I'm feeling low.'

Several minutes later they were walking along the roads, pausing at times to admire flowering shrubs in gardens belonging to other people. Some of the houses had a closed appearance, but as this was a summer weekend most of them were occupied.

They came to the camping-ground which appeared to be full, and as they wandered into the entrance of the large sheltered area they were surprised to see Rolf Warburton standing near the office. The sight of him caused Ivy to draw a sharp breath, and then she moved towards him, almost as if drawn by a magnet.

He turned at her approach. 'Hello. You're taking the air?'

'Yes. And you're arranging for a camping site?'

'Actually I did have that in mind.'

Ivy expressed her surprise. 'Really? I was only joking.'

'But I'm not,' he told her seriously. 'I need to be able to work away from the office and I was considering a caravan, or better still, one of their small units if available.'

Kay said, 'There are many other holiday places—I mean, if this one is over-crowded.'

He sent her a cool glance. 'I have a strong desire to spend the time at Te Awanga.'

Because of Estelle, she thought, then asked, 'Didn't you say you were staying with the Barrons?'

'Only for the weekend. My period from the office gives me a fortnight which begins from next weekend.'

'I'm sure they'd be delighted to have you for that time,' Kay felt prompted to say. 'Do they know this leave is due to you?'

'No, and it's not actually leave in the usual sense of the word. I have work to do.'

'Well, why not tell them?' Kay pursued.

'Because I have no wish to spend two weeks in that house,' he almost rasped with impatience.

'I think I understand.' Kay fell silent, trying to keep her eyes from his broad shoulders and wide chest. His virile body was all male and filled with male needs, her senses told her. The desire to creep into Estelle's bedroom would be overpowering.

Then she almost laughed. Creep? This man? Never. He would simply stride in and throw the bedding to the floor before sweeping the more than willing Estelle into his arms. She would cling to him and there would be silence until he——

Her imagination was cut short by Ivy's words, which almost made Kay freeze from shock. In a voice that was deceptively casual, the older woman said, 'If you have no wish to spend two weeks in the Barron household, how would you feel about spending the time with us? You'd be very welcome.'

CHAPTER THREE

KAY could hardly believe her ears. Ivy, who believed this man wanted her out of Hope House, was deliberately inviting him in! What, for Pete's sake, did she have in mind?

Nor was there any hesitation on Rolf Warburton's part, although he regarded Ivy with undisguised surprise. 'You really mean that?'

'Of course. Arnold Hope was your uncle, wasn't he?'

'Yes, he was my mother's brother.'

'Well then, you should be able to spend time in his house. So will you come?'

'Thank you, I'd like that.'

'But will Estelle like it?' The question slipped from Kay's lips before she could stop it.

His dark brows rose. 'Why the devil should she object?'

Kay bit her lip. 'I'm sorry, I know it's not my business. I just thought that perhaps—you and Estelle——' Her words dwindled.

He made no attempt to enlighten her ponderings. Instead his blue eyes seemed to become penetrating as he said, 'I trust my presence in the house won't disturb you?'

She sent a level glance that belied her inner turmoil. 'Not at all. I'll be so busy in the studio, I won't even know you're there.'

Ivy cut in briskly. 'Well, when may we expect you?'

'I'll be with you in almost a week. Would next Friday be suitable?'

'Yes, of course,' Ivy assured him.

Kay said, 'Have you asked Estelle about sitting for

her portrait?'

'Yes. She's interested, but will make her decision only when she has seen some of your work. I'll admit that surprised me. I thought she'd have seen plenty of it by now. I thought that, living only a few doors from each other, you'd have been friends.'

'Estelle is not interested in friendship with me,' said Kay, knowing he would soon be aware of this.

'Oh? Why not?' The question was snapped abruptly.

Kay shrugged but said nothing. How could she tell him that Estelle had plainly intimated she considered they should vacate Hope House, and that Ivy was a usurper?

To her relief Ivy supplied the answer. 'I'm afraid we're not very socially minded,' she excused. 'We're inclined to keep to ourselves. Kay keeps busy, her painting is really her job, you know, and as for me—well, I haven't wanted anyone else for a long time, at least not since Arnold went,' she added quietly.

'I see.'

Kay felt irritated. You don't see at all, she longed to say. How can you possibly know what Ivy felt for Arnold, or how she's grieved for him? Nor could she see why Ivy had invited this man to stay with them unless—unless his presence gave her the feeling of having Arnold in the house again.

She voiced the question on the way home. 'Why, Ivy? What's on your mind?'

Ivy stared out towards the horizon. 'I suppose you think I'm mad, but actually it was a spur-of-the-moment decision. It was almost as if Arnold whispered in my ear.'

Kay suppressed a smile. 'Oh? What did he say?'

Ivy remained serious. 'It seemed as if he was saying it would enable me to know his nephew better, and after all, it's for only a fortnight, which will soon pass.'

'Yes, I see.' Kay sent Ivy a sharp glance. 'I believe

you're spying out the land. Perhaps you're not being as rash as I thought.'

'Rash? What do you mean by rash? I'm only trying to know Arnold's nephew a little better.'

'You'd like to do that?'

'Of course. Anyone belonging to Arnold is important to me. Besides, it might enable me to learn what he has in mind. So far we've been only guessing at his intentions.'

'Have you thought that once you get him in you might never get him out? He might decide to set himself up as the man of the house?'

'No, I hadn't thought of that.'

'Is there anything in Arnold's will to prevent the owner from moving in, despite your presence?'

Ivy was startled. 'No, there isn't.'

'I notice he needed very little persuasion. What would you do if he married Estelle and brought her to live here?'

Ivy swallowed as she sent Kay a nervous glance. 'I—I don't know. The thought gives me a pain.'

The thought also gave Kay a pain, but she did not admit this to Ivy.

The week passed rapidly while Kay concentrated upon painting gannets. The work was done from photos taken during her visit to the colony at Cape Kidnappers, where it was estimated that between fifteen and twenty thousand birds spent the New Zealand summer.

It had been a memorable trip taken on a tractor-drawn trailer that carried holidaymakers along the beach at the base of vertical, sandy mudstone cliffs. Scarred by perpendicular crevices and diagonal layers, the greyish-white faces rose to heights of about three hundred feet. They were mainly unclimbable, although a few gullies gave access to the plateau lying above the cliffs.

The seven-mile journey was anything but smooth, with rocks and boulders being dodged along the route, while at times stops were made to view earthquake faults made millions of years ago. On the seaward side a colony of terns was passed, and a view given of the gannets at a point known as Black Reef. Later a rest area was reached, and from there it was necessary to climb a track to the plateau for a close view of the main gannet colony.

The long, sharp triangle jutting into the sea was massed with birdlife, and although it was necessary to remain behind the chain boundary of the colony Kay was able to use her camera to advantage.

She discovered the gannets to be surprisingly tame, and by sitting still she found herself rewarded by inquisitive birds that came close while they pecked at the chains, played with feathers or dried fish, preened themselves and even cocked their golden heads to stare at her.

A gannet with a squawking chick beside it was a snap that pleased her, while a bird hovering a short distance overhead was also most satisfying. And now, with the addition of patches of sand, rock or marram grass, these photos gave her numerous studies from which to compose attractive paintings.

By Thursday she had completed six small oil paintings, care having been given to the composition and tone values of each. She placed them in various viewing positions about the room, separating them so that they did not vie with each other, and she was on the verge of calling for Ivy's opinion when the sound of the front doorbell pealed through the house.

Her thoughts flew to Rolf Warburton, whose handsome face had never been far from her mind, intruding to interrupt her concentration upon golden crowns, black-tipped flight feathers against white bodies and black rings around bright eyes. He was not due until tomorrow, so surely he hadn't come a day earlier? If he expected her to spring out to welcome him with cries of gladness he had another think coming, therefore she made no move to go to the door.

But moments later she heard a strong female voice and knew that Ivy had ushered a visitor into the lounge. Kay stood up hastily, placed her oil brushes in a jar of turpentine and took off her painting-smock. She then went out to meet a tall woman of ample proportions and to find herself subjected to a hard scrutiny.

Ivy introduced them. 'This is my cousin's daughter, Kay Carlson. Dear, this is Estelle's mother, Mrs Lexington-Barron.'

Kay sent the visitor a smile that hid her surprise. This woman was Estelle's mother? She searched for a resemblance but could find none. Estelle was slim and delicately beautiful, her flaming hair causing her to stand out in a crowd, whereas her mother was noticeable mainly through a protruding bosom, large hips and an aquiline nose that endowed her with a domineering air. However, her hair still held a shade of red, and her eyes sent a green glint towards Kay.

Ivy said, 'How kind of you to call, Mrs Barron.'

'*Lexington*-Barron, if you don't mind.' The correction came quickly. 'I was a Lexington before I married Mr Barron, you understand. One of the South Island Lexingtons. My forebears arrived in one of the first four ships to reach Christchurch.'

'Oh, I see.' Ivy was slightly taken aback. 'May I offer you a cup of tea or coffee?'

'Tea would be pleasant, thank you,' the visitor conceded graciously. 'However, it's really this young person I've come to see. I'm told she considers herself to be an artist.'

The words sent a shock of surprise through Kay. Was this woman trying to antagonise her? 'I prefer to call myself a painter, rather than an artist,' she responded in cool tones. 'It helps to keep my feet on the ground.'

'What do you mean?' asked the large woman, frowning.

Kay smiled. 'It helps to keep me from imagining my work is better than it really is.'

'I see. Well if it's any good I may be able to help you.'

'How *kind*,' Ivy murmured again.

Kay was interested. 'In what way can you help me, Mrs Lexington-Barron?'

The beak-like nose rose slightly. 'I have friends in high places such as on the City Council, the Harbour Board, the Hospital Board. I could arrange to have your paintings displayed in public buildings. That's if they're up to standard, of course.'

'How—how *very* kind,' Ivy repeated faintly. 'I'll make the tea.' She disappeared towards the kitchen leaving Kay with a strong suspicion she was about to indulge in a fit of the giggles.

Mrs Lexington-Barron continued to stare at Kay, missing no detail of the soft wave in her dark auburn hair, the width of her brown eyes, and the sweetness of her mouth until at last she said, 'Naturally, I'll have to view your work to judge its merit. Where is it?'

'In my studio. If you'll come through to what is really the downstairs bedroom——'

But when they went into the studio the visitor showed little interest in the paintings apart from saying casually, 'Hmm, not bad, not bad at all, but of course you must do larger work for display in public buildings.' Her interest then left the paintings and centred upon the proportions of the room and its outlook. 'So this is the downstairs bedroom. Very suitable, with its built-in wardrobe. Where does that door lead?'

'Into the downstairs bathroom. It's like an en suite.' Kay opened the door to enable her to see the shower, toilet and washbasin, then added, 'Access to it can also be gained from the kitchen.'

'*Most* suitable,' the older woman echoed, gazing up at the fan for expelling steam from the shower. 'How many bedrooms are in this house?'

'Four. Three upstairs with a bathroom and linen cupboards.'

'All double bedrooms?' The green eyes glinted as the question was shot at Kay.

'Yes.' It was then that Kay realised that Mrs Lexington-Barron had not come with philanthropic intentions towards herself. Her suggested help had been merely the excuse for a visit, while her real purpose in coming had been to view the interior of the house.

Within a short time this conviction grew from suspicion to certainty, with little guesswork being necessary to realise that Mrs Lexington-Barron had aspirations towards a match between Estelle and the man who owned Hope House.

Naturally, it would be most suitable to have her daughter living only a short distance along the road where an eye could be kept on the pair. And in her anticipation of the event taking place she had been unable to contain her eagerness to view the interior of the house which she hoped would become Estelle's home.

Nor did this guesswork seem to be at fault when the visitor, apparently having lost interest in Kay's paintings, made her way back to the lounge and from there to the kitchen where Ivy was buttering pikelets made only an hour previously.

Her voice reached Kay's ears. 'Please don't go to any trouble. Ah, fresh pikelets, how *very* nice.' Then, after a pause, 'I see you have a most convenient kitchen—so many cupboards, such good bench space. Indeed, *most* suitable.' Her tone rang with undisguised satisfaction.

Ivy pushed a trolley into the lounge. 'Milk and sugar?'

'Neither, thank you, I'll have lemon,' declared the

visitor.

'I'll fetch it,' said Kay quickly, then hastened to the kitchen where she washed and sliced a lemon. When she returned the visitor was in the midst of confirming all she had suspected.

'It's really a *family* home,' Mrs Lexington-Barron was saying to Ivy. 'It's a place in which to bring up children. You must be finding it much too large for yourself.'

'You're forgetting I have Kay with me,' Ivy pointed out.

'Indeed I am not, and she should also be considered. She's a talented girl. She should be nearer the city where her work can be *shown*. How can she expect to sell her work from Te Awanga?'

Kay smiled at her. 'It's already being shown in shops, but thank you for your interest.'

'I'm glad you appreciate it,' Mrs Lexington-Barron retorted. 'My aim in life is to help people. If there is anything I can do to help, let me do it now. That's my motto.' Her face took on a virtuous expression as she gazed at a point somewhere above Ivy's head.

'Very commendable,' murmured Ivy. 'Another pikelet?'

'Thank you. And I can see that you both need help. I'll not rest until I've seen you both nicely settled.'

Ivy looked puzzled. 'Settled? I'm afraid I don't understand.'

'In a cosy cottage near the city where you'll be close to the shops and all other interests. Someone is sure to know of a place. Believe me, I have contacts.'

'People in higher places?' asked Ivy innocently.

'Exactly. In this life it's not what you know, it's whom you know.' She nodded at the wisdom of her own words.

'I see.' Ivy sent her a level glance. 'But suppose Kay and I have no wish to move nearer the city?'

Mrs Lexington-Barron drew in a deep breath. 'Then legal advice will have to be taken over this ridiculous situation.'

'I beg your pardon?' Ivy's voice had become cold.

'I mean this business of you sitting in a house that is not your own and which is now needed by the rightful owner. Rent free, I believe.' The visitor's voice had risen.

'I've already made sure my position is legal,' said Ivy. 'Arnold's will states quite clearly——'

'I know exactly what Arnold Hope's will states,' the larger woman declared with a hint of vehemence. 'But you can be assured there'll be a loophole somewhere. He was not to know that his nephew would return from Australia and would want to get married. Are you determined to keep a bride and groom from their own home?'

A worried frown appeared on Ivy's face as she said, 'I have yet to be informed that a bride and groom are waiting to move in.'

'Then be assured you'll hear in the near future. Estelle and Rolf are very old friends. Naturally, she's the reason he's returned from Australia.'

Kay was unable to resist a question. 'Are they officially engaged?'

'Not yet, but it'll be announced any day now. Of course, there's always been an *understanding*.' The eyes that rested upon Kay held a clear warning as she added, 'It's better for everybody to know the true situation, don't you think?'

Kay decided to be frank. 'Does one ever understand a true situation?' she asked. 'For instance, you said you'd come here to help me, whereas it's really Estelle and Rolf you have in mind. You're here on *their* behalf, to persuade us to vacate this house.'

Mrs Lexington-Barron assumed a superior air. 'My dear girl, can't you see that it would be better to walk out with dignity, rather than to be pushed out?'

Ivy sighed. 'You're right about that, of course. We'll talk about it when Rolf comes tomorrow.'

The large woman sent her a glare of surprise. 'Did you say tomorrow? I didn't know he'd be with us this weekend. Estelle must have forgotten to tell me.'

'Well as it happens he'll be staying with us.' Ivy smiled. 'He needs time to do some work away from the office, so I invited him to spend it here in Hope House.'

Mrs Lexington-Barron was so aghast she almost lost control. Her eyes glared angrily as she snapped, 'You did *what?*'

'I invited him here,' Ivy repeated. 'I thought he'd like to spend time in the house he'd known as a boy, and that he now owns.'

Icy tones whipped with stinging precision. 'I can see you're a very cunning woman, Mrs Wallace, but if you have any other plans in mind you can forget them.' The glare swept round to embrace Kay. 'And that also applies to you, young woman.'

'What is that supposed to mean?' asked Kay with forced sweetness.

The tones became haughty. 'You are well aware of my meaning, and I'll thank you to remember that Rolf Warburton is almost engaged to my daughter.' Mrs Lexington-Barron placed her cup and saucer on the trolley with a slight clatter, then heaved her bulk from the chair. She then turned to Ivy and said, 'Well, I really must end this interview.'

Ivy looked at her wonderingly. 'Interview? I thought it was a friendly visit to offer help.'

'Exactly. And if you're wise you'll consider my offer to assist you to find other living accommodation—something nearer the city.'

Ivy held out her hand in a formal manner. 'Thank you for your advice, Mrs Lexington-Barron. We'll discuss it further—when the engagement is actually announced.'

'Oh, it will be,' the fond mother declared with confidence.

As the door closed on the visitor Ivy gave a deep sigh of utter weariness. 'I think I'll go to my room and speak to Arnold,' she said. 'He might tell me what to do.'

The first time Ivy had made this statement Kay had been startled into wondering what she meant, but she now knew that Ivy wished to sit and think. And while she pondered she would gaze at Arnold's photo which, she declared, seemed to turn her thoughts in the right direction to solve whatever problem bothered her.

It was Arnold, apparently, who had given her the inspiration to write to Kay. 'There I was in a state of lonely depression,' she told Kay soon after her arrival. 'I just sat on the edge of the bed, gazing at Arnold's photo on the bedside table, when your name shot into my mind. It came from out of the blue, almost as if he'd shouted it at me. And so I wrote, and here you are. So you see dear, I am *not* going dotty.'

How would Arnold advise Ivy this time? Kay wondered as she returned to the studio. Nor had she long to wait for the answer because ten minutes later Ivy came downstairs in a more cheerful mood.

'Well, what did he say?' Kay smiled.

Ivy's face remained serious. 'He told me to sit tight. He reminded me that it was his wish for me to remain in his house, and then he made me feel that the situation would be solved by Rolf himself. If Rolf makes me feel he really wants me out of this house I'll find somewhere else to live because, after all, it is Rolf's house now.'

'In other words, you'll just wait and see what happens.'

'That's right, but in the meantime I'll do something about lunch.'

When Kay woke next morning she was immediately

conscious of a subdued exhilaration that remained with her for the rest of the day. At first she tried to tell herself its cause lay in her recent sales of paintings, and that she was at last attaining her goal of living by her own work, but when she counted the number she had actually sold she knew there was no reason for real excitement.

She also knew that she listened constantly for the sound of the Porsche, although it was late afternoon before it glided into the double carport to be parked beside Ivy's yellow Mini. But before that happened Ivy had prepared an evening meal of Arnold's favourite dishes, and had spent time polishing the furniture in the guest-room.

Kay had watched her from the doorway. 'One would imagine royalty was about to arrive,' she remarked.

Ivy had paused, her grey eyes taking in every detail of Kay's appearance. 'Well, I can see you're ready to greet him. I must say you look lovely.'

It was true. Thought had been given to the dress she would wear, and having divested herself of her painting-smock Kay was now attractively feminine in a sleeveless, full-skirted dress with a low V-neck. The pale apricot silky material hung softly and gave her a glow, while chest bareness was relieved by fine gold chains that glistened in the late afternoon sunlight.

Nor was the effect lost upon Rolf Warburton when he stepped into the hall. He looked at her in silence for several moments, making her feel pleased she had taken extra care with her make-up, and that her newly washed hair had been given a rinse to bring out its golden lights. And then Ivy had led him upstairs towards the guest-room.

Later, as Ivy placed him in Arnold's seat at the head of the table, he reminisced, 'It's a long time since I stayed in this house. In those days my grandparents were alive. The adults slept upstairs while I was put in the downstairs bedroom.'

Kay became aware that his blue eyes were resting upon her. She returned his gaze, wondering if he would like to commandeer the room even now, therefore she said, 'The divan is still in it, if you wish to sleep there. I'm sure Ivy won't mind.'

'Sleep in the studio?' Ivy echoed. 'How could he find comfort in the midst of all your art clutter?' She turned to Rolf, adding earnestly, 'I want you to feel relaxed, and at home.'

'Thank you.' The reply came gravely.

Kay felt a wave of inner hysteria. Had Ivy forgotten that this man owned the place and that he *was* at home? Well, more or less. Hastily she said, 'I was only joking. You'd be most uncomfortable in the studio, especially as there's often a strong smell of turpentine and linseed oil.'

'I don't object to those particular odours, and I'll not disturb your own work too much.'

'Oh?' The remark puzzled her, causing her delicate brows to rise as she waited in silence for enlightenment.

He went on, 'When I slept in that room as a boy, I little dreamt I'd be using it as a workroom in later years.'

She found the statement disturbing. 'Then you do want my studio?'

'Only a corner of it where I can put up a small drawing-board.'

A question shot into her mind. 'Where do you actually live, Rolf?'

'In a flat on the Napier Marine Parade. It's opposite a play area filled with noisy children who don't go back to school before next month, and it's beside a road where the traffic never stops.'

'And so you decided upon a caravan?' Kay asked.

'I can work quite well in a caravan. I decided that Te Awanga would be fairly quiet, a suitable place for uninterrupted work on this particular project, and where the phone is unlikely to plead for short returns to the office.'

'You're working on something secret?' asked Ivy.

The question caused a laugh that transformed his face. '*Secret?* Heavens, no, it's merely a booklet of plans for movable houses. It's being compiled for a firm of builders who construct homes that can be moved on to sections of land. Naturally, they're not the old spacious type of house, but small and modern in design. Nor must they look like little boxes.'

Kay uttered a light laugh. 'I promise not to chatter while you're juggling with bathrooms and kitchens.'

His face became serious. 'If you were the chattering kind I wouldn't be here, much less joining you in the studio.'

Ivy stood up and began to clear the table. 'Why don't you take Rolf into the studio now?' she said to Kay. 'See how it can be arranged to suit you both. Show him all you've been doing this week.'

A sudden reluctance filled Kay. This man who could draw houses that could be built and then moved to another site must surely look upon her own efforts of the past week as being infantile. 'Later, when we've washed the dishes,' she prevaricated in an attempt to put off the viewing moments.

But Rolf stood up and dragged the trolley nearer the table, and in the familiar manner of a permanent resident he began piling the dishes on it. Then, raising a dark eyebrow at Ivy, he said, 'Shall I put the kettle on for coffee?'

Ivy beamed at him. 'Oh yes, please do, it's exactly what Arnold always did.'

Kay glanced at Rolf. Was he aware of the close relationship that had existed between Ivy and his uncle?

The dishes were soon washed and as the last plate was wiped and put away Rolf said, 'You need a dishwasher.'

'Oh, Arnold and I always did them together,' Ivy assured him.

'That doesn't mean you shouldn't enjoy the convenience of such an appliance. I'm surprised he didn't have one installed.' He began to examine the bench then added, 'One could go here, near the plumbing.'

'Really, we don't need a dishwasher,' Ivy protested.

'Nevertheless, you're going to have one. I'll attend to its installation next week.'

Kay felt vaguely troubled as she regarded him thoughtfully. A dishwasher for Ivy and herself—or for Estelle and him?

He went on, 'In the meantime perhaps we could find a tiny corner in the studio for my drawing-board and the easel that holds it. They are in the Porsche, and there are a few other articles to be carried in.' He looked at Kay as though expecting help from her in this task.

She returned his gaze with questions shadowing her brown eyes. Did he really need her help, or was he politely forcing her to be once more confronted by the damage she had caused to his car?

She felt reluctant to look at it, but knew that with the Porsche parked beside the Mini for a fortnight she would have little option but to become accustomed to the sight of it. Therefore she steeled herself and followed him with dragging steps.

When they reached the carport she forced herself to walk round to the passenger side of the car, then drew a deep sigh of relief as she stared almost in disbelief at the smooth perfection of the left wing. The damage had been removed.

'Good as new,' Rolf said. He had been watching her.

'I was afraid to look at it,' she admitted.

'It became an emergency job first thing last Monday morning.'

She gave a short laugh. 'Jumped to do your bidding,

did they? I can't see them bending over backwards if it had been the humble Mini.'

He made no reply as he opened the car and removed a box of technical-drawing instruments which he handed to Kay. He then extracted a roll of sketching-paper and a folded contraption which, when opened out, proved to be his easel.

In the studio it was found that more than the requested tiny corner was necessary to accommodate it, but workable conditions were managed by changing the positions of the dressing-table, the tallboy, and the table Kay used when doing watercolour.

At last Rolf appeared to be satisfied. 'That set-up should be OK,' he said. 'Thank you for allowing me to have space in your holy of holies.' Unexpectedly his hands went to her shoulders to turn her to face him, then his head bent swiftly while his lips brushed hers with a light kiss.

The action startled her, causing her to flush as she stared up at him wordlessly, and as his intent gaze held hers she became aware that the grip of his hands on her shoulders had tightened. Then, before she could protest, his head had lowered again.

This time the kiss was more than a mere brush of the lips. It was a gentle nibbling that caused her pulses to leap, and while her mind sought for words that would acquaint him with her objection to this familiarity, the message seemed unable to pass her lips. Instead her senses were stirred by a sudden excitement as the blood pounded through her veins.

But just as abruptly her head cleared, and as more colour flooded into her face she gasped, 'You've got a colossal nerve.'

'Yes, haven't I just?'

'Please don't imagine you're getting more than *space* in this studio.'

'No? That's a disappointment.'

She took a deep breath that almost hissed with indignation. 'And what's more, I understand you're almost engaged to Estelle Barron.'

The dark brows shot up. 'I am? You surprise me. From where did you learn that intriguing snippet of information?'

'From her mother. She was here yesterday.' Kay glared at him accusingly.

'She was? The dear soul. She said we're engaged?'

Kay hesitated. 'Not exactly, but it was hinted that the announcement was not far away.' Her voice became cold. 'A man who kisses one girl while engaged to another is not to be trusted. In fact, he's despicable.'

His eyes became chips of blue glass. 'Why don't you seek proof before you condemn?'

'Well, you have asked for her portrait to be painted,' she reminded him as this damning piece of evidence swept through her brain.

'So I have! I hope this doesn't mean you'll refuse to do it.'

'I've not yet been assured she'll sit for me.'

'Then I'll have to use persuasion.' He stared at her for several moments in silence, then asked, 'Do you always get uptight when kissed by a man?'

'I am not uptight,' she snapped indignantly.

'No? You could have fooled me. Perhaps you're not kissed often enough to take it in your stride. Have you a boyfriend?'

'That is not your business,' she retorted furiously.

'Which means that the answer is no. Nor is that surprising when one considers you're buried at Te Awanga. You should be in the city where you're fending them off right and left.'

'I've no wish to be fending them off. When I find the man I love I'll have no need to be holding others at bay.'

'Then you haven't found him yet?' The question came softly.

She shook her head. 'Again, that is not your concern.'

He stepped closer to her, his head bent as he looked down into her face. 'Kay, I've no wish to quarrel with you. Can't we begin again?'

She gazed up at him, her eyes wide. 'Yes, I'd like that.'

'Good.' His arms went about her firmly, holding her close to him, and as he found her lips again the kiss held an added depth.

Her head swam lazily as she became gripped by another surge of tingling excitement, but their recent conversation was still too fresh in her mind to allow herself to be carried away, therefore she pushed against his chest and turned her head away. 'No, Rolf, please stop. Isn't this what caused the animosity between us?'

His eyes twinkled. 'On your side only. Personally, I thought we agreed to start again.'

'You know perfectly well I didn't mean to—to start again in—in this manner.'

'What better way could there be?'

'Don't be ridiculous. Besides, I'm not yet sure of the situation between you and Estelle.'

'I'm afraid you'll just have to trust me.'

'Despite the fact that her mother seemed to be very sure of her ground?'

'The dear soul,' he said again, his eyes twinkling.

She waited, giving him the opportunity to say more, but when he remained silent she challenged him, 'I notice you don't deny it. Does that mean you confirm it?'

Again she waited, but before he could answer the sound of the front doorbell came to their ears. Nor did they have to wait long before learning the visitor's identity, because moments later Ivy ushered Estelle Barron into the studio.

CHAPTER FOUR

ESTELLE stood still, her questioning gaze sweeping from Kay to Rolf. The shimmering gold and green dress she wore was cut on lines that emphasised the slimness of her figure, while the folded bodice drew attention to her breasts. The green of the shot silk material complemented her red hair, just as the gold sent a glitter to the eyes that rested upon the tall man.

'Rolf, so you *are* here,' she exclaimed. 'Mother *said* you would be, but I didn't believe her until I saw the Porsche in that—that carport.'

'So what, Stell?' His voice remained casual.

'*Why*, Rolf? Why are you here?' A baleful glance was flicked towards Kay.

Rolf frowned. 'Is it not possible that I have my reasons?'

'But you always come to *us*!' Estelle exclaimed. 'I consider you owe me an explanation, especially as Mother said you have free time due to you.'

'That's not quite correct. I have work with me. See, my easel.'

Its presence registered with Estelle for the first time, and her lower lip quivered slightly as she said, 'You'll be working in here with—with——'

'With Kay,' he supplied. 'But apart from that, I want to go over this house to give it a thorough maintenance check. It's getting on in years and should be examined for borer and patches of wood rot, especially on the south side.'

Estelle's face cleared of its petulance. 'The house—of course. I hadn't thought of the house.'

His tone became dry. 'Then you think about it now,

60

Stell.'

Her face shone with interest. 'Are you saying you might have alterations in mind? But naturally you'd discuss any changes with me.'

'Why would I do that, Stell?' Amusement tinged his voice.

'Because——' She floundered uncertainly for a moment. 'Well, because you've always declared I have such good ideas and can see at once what should be done. Most houses can be improved in some way.

Ivy, who had remained in the doorway during their conversation, now spoke plaintively. 'I don't think Arnold would want his house to be altered. He liked it as it is.'

Estelle's brows rose as she sent the older woman a disdainful look. 'Aren't you forgetting that Arnold is no longer here, and that this house now belongs to Rolf?'

Ivy went on as though she hadn't heard Estelle's remark. 'Arnold's father built it, and it is how Arnold knew it as a boy. If it could have been improved by alterations they'd have been done years ago.'

'That's what *you* think,' Estelle declared uncompromisingly.

Rolf sent her a glowering glance. 'It is also the way I knew it as a boy. Nor would I dream of altering it before I'd lived in it for a period, and had noticed a change that was really necessary.'

A smile broke over Estelle's face. 'Then you do intend to be living in it, and that means——' She broke off as she sent questioning glances from Kay to Ivy.

Kay felt her spirits drop. 'That means he expects us to begin looking for somewhere else to live.' Her voice became cool as she turned to Rolf. 'Isn't that so, Mr Warburton?'

His jaw tightened slightly as he glared at her coldly. 'In the field of conclusions you appear to be several jumps ahead of yourself. At the moment I'm more than happy with living conditions in my flat on Napier Parade, but if I'm grabbed by the whim to live here on a more permanent basis, I shall move in. I'm sure a good lawyer would find the right for me to do just that.'

Ivy clapped her hands and beamed at him. 'I would be so pleased for you to do so,' she said happily.

'Thank you.' He sent another cold glare towards Kay. 'It's nice to know I'd be welcomed by at least one of the present residents.'

Kay looked at him wordlessly, searching for an answer. Would this same bright lawyer also find means of pushing Ivy and her out of the house? And then Rolf's voice put the question out of her mind as he spoke to Estelle.

His voice still cool, he said, 'The real purpose of your visit still eludes me, Stell, unless it was to arrange sitting times for your portrait.'

She snatched at the suggestion. 'The portrait—yes, of course, that was it. But first I'd like to see——'

'Samples of Kay's work in the portrait field? There's an example, and there's the subject.' He nodded from Ivy to the painting that hung on the wall.

Estelle's eyes went from one to the other in a long scrutiny until at last she said, 'I must admit it's not bad.' Then she smiled up into his face. 'Rolf dear, it's so sweet of you to want a portrait of me. It—it tells me *so much*. Yes, *of course* I'll sit. When may we begin?' she added, turning to Kay with a show of enthusiasm.

Kay hesitated, knowing that she now had no desire to begin even a pencil sketch of Estelle. 'Working conditions will be cramped,' she demurred. 'I'm not sure that I can manage——'

'Perhaps it could be done in the lounge,' suggested Ivy.

Estelle became petulant. 'No, I want to sit near Rolf while he's working. Besides, I'm surprised you're not afraid of paint being dropped on *Arnold's* carpet,' she flashed at Ivy with a clear hint of sarcasm.

'Kay's a clean worker,' Ivy protested indignantly. 'She puts newspaper down and—and——'

'That won't be necessary,' Rolf cut in sharply as he began to take control of the matter by moving a chair. 'The model can sit here, with Kay's easel about here, and this small table can be placed here to hold her box of oil paints and the palette when she's mixing colours for skin tones.' He paused, turning to Kay for approval of these arrangements.

Kay, however, did not approve. She felt irritated, and she met his gaze with a question swimming about in her mind.

'Well?' he asked impatiently. 'That's OK, isn't it?'

'No, it is not OK.' Then despite herself the question came out into the open. 'Am I right in assuming you're dead keen to have your *friend* sitting beside you while you work?'

'Of course you're right,' Estelle cut in happily, a small smile of satisfaction playing about her lips.

Kay ignored her as she continued to glare at Rolf. 'In fact, you're so keen, it doesn't matter a hoot if I'm forced to work under cramped conditions.'

His jaw tightened but he said nothing.

Kay went on, 'Surely you can understand that the job of painting a portrait, getting a likeness, is difficult enough in itself without having other hassles attached to it.'

'Other hassles—such as what?' he demanded.

'Close up and distance,' she snapped. 'I like to be able to stand back and examine the work, but as you're having me placed I'm stuck too close to the canvas.'

Warming to her protest, she was gripped by the desire to hit out at him. How dared he come into her studio and dictate about where her easel should be placed? And how could she paint a competent portrait with the model simpering at him like a moonstruck twit?

She continued, 'I even like to move the easel, placing it beside the model so that I can see them together, and I like to stand with my back to them while I look at them both while holding a mirror so that I can see them over my shoulder. That's when the errors show up.'

His reaction to her outburst was surprising. A grin spread over his face as he said, 'You sure know what you want.'

'It's what I must have when doing a portrait.'

'So what have you in mind?'

'I shall do it in the lounge as Ivy suggested, and if your *friend* continues to object I shall not do it at all. Is that understood?'

Rolf's blue eyes held a spark of amusement as they rested upon her. 'The lady appears to have a mind of her own,' he drawled. 'Does she always stand up and fight those within reach?'

'When the occasion demands it,' Kay snapped back at him, her chin uplifted. 'At least she does not intend to be bullied. You may own this house, Mr Warburton, but you can't come in and tell me what to do, especially when it means pushing me into a corner to paint a portrait. Personally, I think you've got a nerve.'

Estelle's voice came angrily. 'You're the one with the nerve, Kay Carlson. You've no right to speak to Rolf in that manner. It's a wonder he doesn't throw you both out of this house right now. Mother says he has every right.'

'Shut up, Stell,' Rolf snapped furiously. 'Make your arrangements for the sittings and then I'll walk you home.'

She frowned at him. 'I'm not sure that I want her to do it. There are other people in this district who can paint a portrait, and believe me, if it were not for the fact that you're here——'

'Just do as I say.' Rolf's tone was curt.

Estelle turned to Kay and spoke in a dictatorial manner. 'I shall come tomorrow afternoon at two o'clock.'

Kay's voice remained cool. 'I'm afraid that time will not be suitable.'

'Oh? Why not?' Arrogance tinged the question.

'Because at that time direct sunlight will be in the room. It causes endless changes of light and shadows. You may come at ten o'clock and I'll work until twelve, with rest-breaks, of course.'

'Very well, and after that Rolf will take me for a jogging-run along the beach.' Estelle flashed a provocative smile at him.

'I doubt it,' said Kay calmly.

Estelle sent her a piercing stare. 'Why not? Why shouldn't Rolf take me jogging along the beach?'

'Because the tide will be high by midday,' Kay returned sweetly. 'You'd be struggling through deep shingle and most amusing to watch.' She giggled at the thought.

Rolf gave a short laugh, then said hastily, 'Let's go, Stell.'

'Don't call me Stell,' she almost hissed at him. 'You know my name is Estelle. It means a star,' she added loftily.

'Something glittering but out of reach,' he retorted drily.

'That's right.' The provocative smile flashed again.

Kay's eyes narrowed as she watched them walk along the short concrete drive. 'I believe she's playing hard to get,' she said to Ivy. 'One minute she's sending him come-hither looks, the next minute she's warding him off.'

'It's possible. Personally, I believe he's annoyed with her,' Ivy returned. 'Just look at those long strides. She has to almost run to keep up with him.'

'Annoyed with her or with me?'

'That question worries you?' Ivy asked casually.

'Not at all,' retorted Kay loftily. 'Although I have a strong suspicion that the tranquillity of our lives is about to be shattered.'

Ivy's eyes held a speculative gleam. 'Tranquillity? Are you saying you're already aware of an inner turmoil caused by that devastating man?'

'Certainly not.' Kay did her best to sound scornful but found difficulty in convincing even herself.

'Well, I suppose that's the last we'll see of him this evening,' remarked Ivy, sending her a sly glance.

'He can stay with her all night as far as I'm concerned,' Kay retorted with a slight shrug.

'That's a lie,' Ivy accused her quietly.

Kay failed to meet her eyes as she changed the subject. 'I'd prefer to think about tomorrow. Now then, if I place the model's chair at this end of the room near the fireplace, the light will fall on her face from that window.' She carried a small comfortable chair across the room.

Ivy said, 'You mean to have her looking towards the studio door?'

'Yes. She'll then be able to see Rolf at his work without having to fidget in her efforts to do so.'

'I must say you're being most accommodating.'

'Not really. I'm merely assuring myself of a sitter who will remain still.' She went into the studio and returned with a light wooden contraption which she expanded and set up a short distance from the chair.

Ivy said, 'Ah, your folding easel. I haven't seen you use it since I sat for you.'

'It's lighter than the studio easel, therefore it's easier to move and place beside the model when I want to view them together.' She then returned to the studio twice, returning the first time with a small table, and then with her box of oil paints.

Ivy watched as she opened the box and extracted

various tubes. 'Something tells me that Estelle Barron will not prove to be your favourite model. I hope your dislike of her won't affect your work, and don't try to tell me you feel impartial towards her.'

'Actually, she's a most attractive model, and normally I'd be delighted to paint her portrait. It's just her attitude towards us that infuriates me, to say nothing of her obvious desire to get us out of this house. However, I'll do my best.'

'To please—*him*?'

'Definitely not. It's because of pride in my work.' She paused, then demanded defiantly, 'Why should I aim to please him?'

'Why, indeed?' said Ivy.

Kay felt irritated. 'If you imagine I'm moonstruck by this man, you're mistaken. To be honest, I'm not sure that I trust him.'

'What do you mean?'

'He's being too nice.'

'Of course he's nice. He's Arnold's nephew, isn't he?'

'That fact does not cause me to view him through rose-tinted spectacles.'

'You're saying I'm being deliberately blind?'

'It's possible.'

'I don't know why you're taking this attitude about Rolf.'

'Perhaps it's because I damaged his car and he hasn't said a word about it, apart from letting me know the garage people were quick with the repair job.'

'If you expected him to keep harping on about it, it would be because you're still feeling guilty about the incident. But I suspect Rolf has put it behind him.'

Kay looked doubtful. 'Maybe, but it's his charm that makes me suspicious. I think he intends to work round you until you're like putty in his hands.'

'I don't understand.'

'OK, let me spell it out this way. Instead of *asking*

you to leave, he'll be so nice you'll hand the place over just to please him.'

'You're mistaken,' declared Ivy firmly. 'I'm not likely to forget Arnold's wishes.'

'You'll reach the stage of imagining it is Arnold's wish. And besides, Arnold's wishes might be one thing while the law might be something else. I really think you should have another talk to your solicitor about your situation. You must be absolutely sure that Rolf can't put you out.'

'I feel sure he'll respect Arnold's wishes,' sighed Ivy.

'Perhaps, or perhaps not. However, you must remember that Arnold loved you, whereas this man does not. And while Arnold was gentle and kind to you, his nephew has a tough streak below the surface.'

A slight cough caused her to swing round and face Rolf who leaned nonchalantly in the doorway. 'Most interesting,' he drawled.

'How long have you been eavesdropping?' she demanded, angered by the flush she knew to be staining her cheeks.

'Long enough.' Then his voice hardened. 'Why do you accuse me of eavesdropping? I understood I was a guest in this house. I merely walked in the back door which had been left open.'

She stared at him in silence while searching for words. How much had he heard?

Ivy came to the rescue. 'Kay is only concerned on my account.'

He cut in, his voice still harsh. 'Kay is more concerned on her own account. She fears the loss of her cosy studio and the general upheaval of a move that would interfere with her peaceful days of pleasant painting.'

Kay interrupted him angrily. 'You've got it all wrong, Rolf Warburton. You've been listening to Estelle—and her mother.' She took a deep breath then rushed on, 'In fact I'm surprised to see you home so early. The moon has risen, the tide is low, so isn't now the time to take Estelle tramping through the shingle?' The thought held so little romance it made her giggle.

'You must have your small joke,' he growled. 'As it happens, I came home early to talk to you.'

'You did?' His words amazed her.

'As you say, the tide's low. It's down to the fine gritty part where walking is easy, so shall we go?'

'You're asking—*me*—to go for a walk along the beach?'

'Of course he is,' Ivy cut in impatiently. 'Are you getting deaf, dear? Put on a warm jacket because the sea breeze can be chilly.'

Kay obeyed without realising she was doing so, and minutes later found herself crossing the road towards the shingle that bordered the upper reaches of the shore. In walking its unstable surface she flung out an arm to help her balance, then instantly found her hand taken in a firm grip that generated a ball of fire in her palm and sent tingles shooting up her arm.

The impact caused a small gasp to escape her, and she wondered if he had noticed the unexpected warmth in their handclasp; but when she glanced at him she found his face to be a pale, expressionless blur in the moonlight.

He led her down to the smoother part of the beach near the water's edge where the curl on the tiny lapping waves betrayed an undertow. To their right the moon threw a glow across the water, while across the curve of the bay the lights of Napier twinkled like a distant cluster of diamonds.

At first she felt strangely tongue-tied as questions swung about in her mind. Why did he wish to talk to her? Why hadn't he done so at home? And then the reason for this became clear as his deep tones voiced questions of his own.

'Tell me about Ivy,' he said abruptly.

'Ivy?' She was startled. 'You've brought me out here to talk about her?'

'That's right. Would you say she was fond of my uncle?'

'*Fond* of him? Huh, that's an understatement.'

'You're implying she was in love with him?'

Kay became wary. She had no wish to discuss Ivy, especially her private emotions concerning Arnold, therefore she said, 'Why not ask her yourself?'

'It's rather difficult to do so.'

'Why do you want to know these things?'

'Because I'd like to know the truth of the affair. Nor have I any wish to upset her by appearing to pry into the emotional state that existed between them.'

'The emotional state . . .' Kay fell silent, suddenly conscious of the tension in her own emotional state while walking beside this tall handsome man whose aura seemed to reach out and touch her. His magnetic personality sent quivers through her entire nervous system, and as she recalled the feel of his lips on hers a hot flush crept over her body, causing her to put more space between them lest he became aware of her tension.

But at the moment he was remaining completely casual towards her as he asked, 'Can you blame me for wanting to know the truth? It's obvious she meant a great deal to Arnold, so was his regard for her reciprocated, or was he in fact merely manipulated by her?'

'Ah, you've been listening to Mrs Lexington Barron.'

'Believe me, I'm more interested in listening to you.'

Kay walked in silence for several long moments while she pondered the question. Ivy might not thank her for discussing her affair with Arnold, but perhaps it would be wiser for her to do so, and, coming to a decision, she took a deep breath and said, 'I know only what Ivy has revealed in unguarded moments when she found herself longing to talk about Arnold.'

He said nothing, waiting for her to continue.

'Ivy and Arnold met each other when they were both in dire need of someone to heal the wounds of broken marriages. Within a short time they came to love each other deeply, and for ten years Ivy's life revolved round Arnold. Now it revolves round his memory—or his ghost, because sometimes I wonder if he's very far away from her.'

'You're saying she still feels close to him.'

'If you're sufficiently observant you'll see this for yourself.'

'What made you come to stay with her?'

'She needed a companion to help her cope with the emptiness.'

'But surely a companion nearer her own age would have been more suitable.'

'I'll admit I thought so at the time, but when I discussed it with my mother she said that if Ivy wanted me to be with her, I should go. Also, I'd been made redundant at the time.' She told him about her previous employment in an art department.

'So your job was selling art materials?'

'Sometimes I demonstrated how to use those materials, mainly because I loved to handle them. Before starting the job I'd spent a long period at art school, and for years I'd been going to night art classes. Then, when Ivy suggested selling paintings to tourists the temptation to try and make my own way in the art field proved to be too great.'

'There was no other reason for coming to Ivy?'

'No.' She looked at him sharply. 'What other reason are you trying to imagine?'

He continued to stare straight ahead. 'Well, an affair of the heart, perhaps? It's possible you'd had a quarrel with someone—er—important to you and desired a new beginning in a different district. In other words, you'd run away.'

She laughed. 'Wrong, Mr Warburton. Entirely wrong. My mind is free of all men, and in the meantime I intend it to remain that way.'

'I'm glad of that.'

Her brows rose. 'Really? Why should my emotional state interest you, especially when you have Estelle the star twinkling so close at hand?' Be careful, she warned herself. That was distinctly catty.

His next words came soothingly to her jaded spirit. 'It was just that I wondered why a lovely girl like you should bury herself at Te Awanga.'

Her mind snatched at his words. *A lovely girl.* Was he sincere in stating he believed her to be a lovely girl? Aloud she said, 'There's no need for flattery, Rolf Warburton. Keep it for someone who'll lap it up.'

'There's no need for you to be jealous of Estelle,' he said.

'*Jealous?*' She almost choked on the word. 'That'll be the day.' Or had the day come? She asked herself with a sense of shock. Was she indeed jealous of Estelle and her close association with this man who seemed to have the power to send her pulses racing? It was an association close enough for him to desire a portrait of the beautiful redhead, she reminded herself with a pang.

'How old are you?' he asked abruptly.

'Twenty-three, if it is any of your business, and it seems to me that while you brought me out to learn about Ivy you now know all about *me*.'

He ignored her angry outburst by saying, 'I'm eight years your senior, which makes me old enough to know that Ivy must not spend the rest of her life with a ghost.'

'She must be given time to get over her grieving.'

'I mean her mind must be given fresh fields to explore.'

'Ah, then you do mean to put her out of Arnold's house.'

'I didn't say that.'

'Will it be through the law, or through the help of Mrs Lexington-Barron's "friends in higher places"?' It was a difficult to keep the sarcasm from her voice.

He stood still, then swung round to face her. 'Do you know, there are times when I could shake the devil out of you?'

'Then we'd better go back before you're tempted to dip my head in the waves twice and take it out once.'

'I'll admit the thought of doing so has occurred to me,' he gritted at her as he took a step closer. 'However, I'm assailed by an even greater temptation, one that could prove to be an effective punishment for some of those pithy remarks that are flung at me all too easily.'

Without warning he snatched her to him, his warm mouth finding hers before she could turn her head away, and despite the force of his kiss it deepened further into something that was even more disturbing. The hand that had previously sent tingles up her arm now held the back of her head in a firm grip, while his other arm pressed her against the length of his body.

A small fire began to glow somewhere below the region of her navel, the sparks from it shooting into her bloodstream and causing her senses to become inflamed. And although she fought against the rising sensation of being lifted into the air, she found herself almost unable to control the reeling dizziness of her mind.

Nevertheless she steeled herself into keeping her response to a minimum, and it was only sheer willpower that prevented her arms from creeping about his neck. He can think I'm cold, she decided. It might make him think twice about repetitions of this performance.

Suddenly he was staring down at her, the moonlight emphasising the harsh lines about his mouth. 'You don't like being kissed by a man?' he demanded, frowning.

'Not when that man is almost engaged to somebody else,' she reminded him. 'Nor does it amuse me to be treated as a cheap side-encounter. I understand you've come back to New Zealand only because of Estelle.'

'Where in hell's name did you hear that morsel of nonsense?'

'It was hinted at by one who shall be nameless.'

He laughed, his amusement transforming his face. 'Ah, the identity is easy to guess. It was hinted at by she who has friends in higher places?'

It was Kay's turn to laugh, her amusement further easing the tension between them, and as they turned to retrace their steps she said, 'Well, is it true? Did you return to New Zealand because of Estelle?'

'Certainly not. I came because I was offered a partnership in a good firm and in an area I'd known and loved as a boy. This whole area is full of nostalgia for me.'

'You allowed nostalgia to dictate your life?'

'Let's say it was part opportunity and part nostalgia which has a strange power of its own.'

'Then if you realise the intensity of nostalgia you will understand what leaving Hope House could do to Ivy, and how it could send her into a state of depression.'

He said nothing for several moments, then ignored her reference to Ivy and Hope House by changing the subject. 'They travel overseas, they see the world and its wonders of bright lights and all it has to offer, but unless they throw down roots in some place they always come home to these small islands with their green pastures and rocky shores.'

'Then you didn't throw down roots by becoming involved with an Australian girl?'

'No.' The reply came abruptly.

'I'm sorry, I shouldn't have asked such a personal question, but you did ask questions about me. In fact you know quite a lot about me, while I know nothing

about you.' She was unaware that her voice held a tinge
of grievance.'

His laugh was short and derisive. 'I can hardly believe
you'd be even remotely interested.'

She felt nettled. 'Why do you say that?'

'Because of your obvious lack of interest in being
kissed by me,' he snapped, his voice betraying a barely
concealed irritation. 'It almost amounted to—dislike.'

She digested his words, longing to tell him that she
was interested. The warm glow generated by his kiss had
continued to swim in her veins, and suddenly she knew
that despite herself she was more than interested in this
man. She longed to know everything about him: his
likes and dislikes, his moments of gladness and
disappointment, his hopes and failures. The knowledge
shocked her into silence until at last she said in a low
voice, 'You're quite mistaken. I am interested.'

'You have a strange way of showing interest in any
embraces that might come from me,' he said tersely.
'Cool, is what I'd call you.'

His words caused her to rake her mind for a suitable
answer, one that would not betray her real attraction
towards him, therefore she said, 'Don't you see? My
interest lies in a different direction.' Then, choosing her
words carefully, she went on, 'Would it surprise you to
learn that, through Ivy, I feel I know Arnold quite well?
So why should it be strange for me to be interested in
knowing a little about his nephew's life?'

He said, 'There's very little to tell, apart from the fact
that it's been monotonously tied to the study of
architecture and all that goes with it. At least, until I
reached the stage of being able to step into an assured
position.'

'Your father is also an architect?'

'No. He owns a construction company, and a very
successful one because he's now a wealthy man. He had
hopes of handing the reins to me while he spent time

playing with his yacht, but it was all too easy.'

'What do you mean?'

'There was no challenge in taking over the ready-made firm that had become established by his efforts. My ultimate aim is to build something by my own efforts.'

'He must have been disappointed in your decision to return to New Zealand,' she said, guessing at the angry scenes between Rolf and his father.

'Disappointed? He was raving mad, but eventually he realised that I needed the satisfaction of spreading my own wings. Then, when the question of Uncle Arnold's house came to light, he agreed I needed a period to examine it and decide what I should do about the property.'

'The question being whether you'd live in it, sell it, or allow Ivy to remain in it?'

'That's right, although I didn't expect to discover Arnold's ghost still in residence. His wishes are not demands. They merely give her the option to live there if she wishes to do so. I believed there'd be no trouble in moving her to alternative accommodation.'

'But then you don't know Ivy. She clings.'

'She could be moved into my flat on Napier Parade. Expenses would be taken care of, just as they are now.'

Kay sighed. 'Just give her time. It won't go on for ever. Ivy really needs something to occupy her mind, something to help push Arnold's image into the background, and then the house will be all yours. To live in with Estelle,' she added, the words slipping out before she could stop them.

'I'm not sure that I'm keen to swap Ivy for Mrs Lexington-Barron,' he remarked lightly.

'Hope House is well named,' she went on as though he hadn't spoken. 'You hope to prise Ivy out of it, while she hopes to remain in it. Mrs Lexington-Barron hopes to see her daughter nicely settled in it, while Estelle hopes to become the mistress of it.'

'And you? What are your hopes?' The words came softly as he turned to face her.

'My aspirations have nothing to do with Hope House,' she flashed at him.

'You must have some special desires,' he persisted.

'Only to become successful as an artist,' she declared in a voice that rang with determination. 'I've been grateful for the studio-space Hope House has provided, but that won't last for ever because in this life nothing stays the same.'

'You have no aspirations towards marriage? The thought of becoming a mother doesn't appeal to you?' Again he spoke softly.

'I'll face that question when I meet the right person.'

'Someone who doesn't kiss you while almost engaged to another?'

'You've taken the words right out of my mouth,' she shot at him, then hurried towards the shingle lining the upper reaches of the shore. But as she stepped into the area of loose stones she overbalanced and almost fell.

He flung out a hand to snatch at her arm. 'Not so fast or you'll be flat on your face.'

She skipped aside with a sharp exclamation. 'I'm OK, thank you.'

He grabbed her arm again, this time holding it firmly. 'You will allow me to assist you, Miss Independent?'

'It's you who need the assistance—in making the right decision,' she snapped at him.

'Which decision have you in mind?' he asked.

She made no reply. Instead she wrenched her arm from his grasp, then fled over the stones towards the road. And as she ran home she told herself she was a fool to become agitated over whatever decision this man might choose to make. If it became necessary for Ivy and her to leave Hope House, well, that would be that and they would have to face up to the situation.

As for his decision to marry Estelle, that was something about which she couldn't care less. Or could she? No, of course she couldn't. She must be mad to be even wondering about it. However, she realised that in considering the problem of the house he was also renewing his old association with Estelle. His request for a portrait of her proved that to be a fact, didn't it?'

CHAPTER FIVE

KAY was almost out of breath when she flung herself through the back door that led into the kitchen.

Rolf was close behind her. 'We'll have coffee,' he stated, looking at her flushed cheeks.

'Man of the house already?' she teased.

He ignored the remark by looking in the lounge where only a standard lamp broke the darkness. 'Where's Ivy?' he asked.

'I suppose she's gone to bed. Didn't you notice the bright light shining from her room?'

'I was too busy chasing after you to notice anything,' he growled. 'Do you always make a habit of running away from a man whose intentions are nothing but pure and honourable?'

She returned his banter. 'Ah, but how can a poor girl be sure?' Then, placing three coffee mugs on a tray, she changed the subject by saying, 'Ivy will be reading in bed, but I feel sure she'd enjoy a hot drink. If we take ours upstairs we can have it together.'

'Very well.' He examined the flat, crisp, spicy cookies she took from a jar, then bit into one. 'Hmm, these are delicious.'

'Arnold's favourite hokey-pokey biscuits,' she informed him drily. 'You'd better understand that here everything revolves round Arnold.'

He became silent as he carried the tray and its three steaming mugs up the stairs.

Kay gave a light tap on the bedroom door which was ajar. 'May we come in?' she called.

'Of course, dear.'

They went in to find Ivy sitting up in bed, a book on

79

her lap, and while the shaded lamp softened her features, making her look younger, it also sent a bright glow over the silver-framed photograph on the bedside table.

'Ah, coffee, how kind of you to bring it up to me,' she exclaimed. 'Arnold and I always enjoyed a cup in the evening. This was his room, you know,' she told Rolf.

'I remember it as my grandparents' room,' said Rolf, his eyes moving from the walk-in wardrobe to the en suite with its toilet facilities. They rested momentarily on the photograph, then went to the wide windows where the long drapes had been left undrawn. 'Do you always sleep with the blinds up and the curtains open?' he asked as he sipped his coffee.

'Yes. Arnold liked them that way. When the light was out we used to lie—I—I mean—he enjoyed looking out at the stars.' Ivy had turned a deep pink.

Watching her, Kay was filled with sympathy. Dear Ivy, that was a slip, she thought.

'You slept together?' asked Rolf blatantly.

Ivy sent him a defiant glare. 'Of course we slept together. We loved each other. Didn't Mrs Lexington-Barron tell you I'm no better than I should be?'

'I have not discussed the matter with her,' retorted Rolf coolly.

'Hmm. Well, give her time. One day when we happened to meet in the corner shop she asked why only one bedroom light seemed to burn at night.' Ivy lifted the photo from the bedside table, kissed it, then pressed it against her breast. 'I was very proud to have won Arnold's love. I couldn't care less about what anybody thought or said.' Her eyes filled with tears as she replaced the photo on the table.

Kay said hastily, 'Don't upset yourself, Ivy. Is your coffee OK? Not too strong?'

'It's lovely, thank you dear.' Ivy sniffed, reaching for

a tissue in a box on the table. 'I know I'm a fool but I—I can't seem to help myself.' She turned to Rolf. 'You see, Arnold and I had become so very close to each other.'

'I understand,' he said gruffly.

Ivy shook her head. 'I doubt it. It's something you can't possibly understand unless you've been close to a person.' Her grey eyes regarded Rolf intently. 'Have you ever been close to anyone?'

Kay found herself waiting for his answer, but when it came it told her nothing.

'Not in the way you mean,' he said, then sidled away from that particular issue by asking, 'Was my uncle ill for a long time?'

'For as long as it took that wretched leukaemia to do its rotten work,' said Ivy vehemently. 'I nursed him until he was beyond my skill, until the time came when hospital was necessary . . .' The words ended because she was unable to speak and as the tears fell she pressed a tissue to her eyes.

Rolf took several paces about the room, then spoke to Ivy in a brisk manner. 'This conversation is upsetting you. I think you'd be wise to have another read to clear your mind of the sad memories, and then you must try to sleep.'

'You're right,' admitted Ivy. 'And I must also learn to pull myself together. I'm sorry for being such an idiot.'

'You're clinging to the past,' Rolf admonished. 'You'd be wiser to put that photo out of sight. It's a constant reminder of all you've lost.'

Her eyes widened as she gaped at him in dismay. 'Put Arnold's photo away? Oh, no, I couldn't possibly do that. It means so much to me. It means he's *with* me.'

He waited in grim silence until she had finished the rest of her coffee, and it was then that Kay sensed his displeasure. She felt uneasy as she followed him downstairs, and as he placed the tray on the bench she became even more aware of the tightness of his jaw and the hard line about his mouth. Nor did she have to wait long before his anger rose to the surface.

'Well, that was a cunning ruse,' he snapped crisply.

She turned to stare at him. 'Cunning ruse? What are you talking about?'

'You thought you'd try the old sympathy trick, eh?'

She frowned, trying to fathom his meaning, but could only shake her head in perplexity. '*Sympathy* trick? What do you mean?'

'You know what I mean.'

'No. What you're getting at is a complete mystery to me.'

His mouth twisted into a mirthless smile. 'I dare say you can work it out for yourself. I'm sure you're smart enough.'

She became frustrated. 'No, I can't, so please tell me what's bugging you. Surely it's not too much to ask.'

'Very well.' He paused, frowning, then went on in a hard voice. 'It was your suggestion to take coffee upstairs, was it not?'

'Yes. So what?'

'You knew perfectly well that I'd see Arnold's photo prominently displayed with Ivy stretched beside it.'

'She was not! She was sitting up reading,' Kay snapped.

His tone became accusing. 'You wanted me to see her alone and forlorn in the room she'd shared with Arnold.'

'You're being ridiculous,' she exclaimed, her anger rising.

'Taking the coffee to her was a deliberate ploy to stir my sympathy,' he stated with conviction.

'How dare you accuse me of such—such *duplicity*,' she hissed in a fury, her brown eyes widening with distress.

'And in doing so you hoped to gain your own ends,' he pursued relentlessly.

'*Ends*? What sort of ends?'

'Ends such as seeing the last of me. You hoped I'd feel so sorry for Ivy I'd just vanish and forget all about this house. I'd leave the pair of you to live in it without any further complications. That performance Ivy put on must have surpassed your expectations.'

'You must be out of your mind,' she exploded.

'It's possible,' he admitted gloomily. 'But I think not.'

She controlled her temper as a thought struck her. 'Aren't you forgetting one small fact?'

'What would that be?' His tone had become bleak.

'It concerns Ivy's—performance. If I remember correctly, it was you who had the gall to bring up the subject of sharing the bed. You actually asked her if they'd slept together. Naturally she became upset.'

He scowled. 'You've the temerity to blame me for her tears?'

'Of course I blame you. It's a subject I've never once mentioned to her. I wouldn't dream of doing so.'

'Because you're so naïve you didn't realise they were sleeping together?'

'Don't be *stupid*. Of course I knew they were sleeping together. Why shouldn't they sleep together? They were both free to do so, they loved each other, and that's the reason I never mentioned it to Ivy. I knew the memory would be a poignant one. How could it be otherwise? Or are you too insensitive to appreciate that?'

'Ivy's fortunate to have someone to champion her cause,' he said. 'However, I still consider you had a purpose in persuading me to go upstairs with the coffee.'

'I don't recall persuasion being necessary.'

'That's because I went without realising——.'

She finished the sentence for him. 'That I had a

deliberate plan to enlist your sympathy?' She glared at
him, her chin held high, her face flushed with anger.
'Thank you, thank you very much indeed for that slur
on my integrity.'

He returned her glare from beneath lowered brows.
'Touches you on the raw, does it?'

'I'd be lying if I denied it. But if that's your opinion
of me, well, so be it.' She turned and went towards the
door before he could see the tears that almost blinded
her. Then, blinking rapidly, she reached the stairs
before they had begun to roll down her cheeks. *Idiot*,
she chided herself. Why worry about what he thinks?

Next morning the clear sky promised another warm day.
The sea glistened beneath the rising sun, and as Kay
gazed across the sparkling expanse she reminded herself
that Estelle would arrive at ten o'clock.

Her anger of the previous evening had evaporated
during the night, and she was now ready to do her best
in producing a portrait of the beautiful redhead, one
that would please Rolf Warburton who apparently
desired to have her likeness hanging on his wall.

No doubt the time would come when it would be a
feature in the lounge downstairs, she thought, conscious
of a twinge of bitterness, but this thought was brushed
aside before it could expand into an overwhelming
depression because today she wished to feel cheerful.
Today she would begin on a task which must not be
affected by a black mood.

She was a little later than usual in going down for
breakfast, mainly because she had overslept after a
disturbed night when Rolf's blue eyes seemed to glow at
her through the intense darkness. During those wakeful
moments she had turned her head to stare up at the
stars, watching them as Ivy and Arnold had watched
them through the uncurtained windows. How long
would it be before Rolf and Estelle gazed up at them,

possibly from that same double bed?

'Good morning, dear,' said Ivy brightly as Kay entered the kitchen. 'Rolf has had his breakfast. He's in the studio already at work.'

Kay spread marmalade on buttered toast. 'I'll not disturb him. Most of what I need has already been put in the lounge.' Then to herself she added in silent gratitude, And thank goodness for that much. I've no wish to talk to *that man*. The less I see of him the better. I'll keep out of the lounge until about a quarter to ten.

But she had forgotten her painting smock which still hung in the wardrobe at the far end of the room. To fetch it she had to pass Rolf, who worked at the wide drawing-board which rested upon its special stand, and as she crossed the room politeness forced her to say, 'Good morning.'

He turned to regard her gravely, his face unsmiling. 'Good morning. You're ready for the fray?'

'Fray?' She frowned. 'I'm not expecting a fight of any sort.'

'Estelle can be difficult.'

'Why should she be difficult? I'm the one wielding the brushes and the one faced with the problem of getting a likeness. She has only to sit still.'

'She'll expect you to make her look quite beautiful.'

'That won't be difficult. Surely you know that she *is* beautiful.'

'I know there are times when her face is marred by a sulky expression which I have no wish to see on the portrait.'

'Are you afraid I'll put it there, perhaps to annoy you because last night you questioned my integrity?'

He made no reply, although his jaw tightened.

She went on, 'You have no need to worry, Mr Warburton. I'll do my best to portray your—fiancée's beautiful features, although whether the result is a success or a failure remains to be seen.'

'I'd like Mrs Lexington-Barron to be pleased with it,' he admitted bluntly. 'She's the one who'll be critical.'

The words surprised her until she grasped the reason behind them. 'I understand. It'll make her realise your intentions are serious. It'll galvanise her into action. She'll find a place for Ivy to move into before the paint on the portrait is dry.' Her brown eyes swept him with a look of disgust. 'And *you* dare to accuse *me* of duplicity.'

'You don't understand,' he said furiously from behind clenched teeth. 'Perhaps I should explain.'

'There's no need for you to bother,' she cut in. 'I'm not so dumb I can't recognise *real* cunning when it stares me in the face.' Then she laughed because instinct told her she had now triumphed over last night's little spate, and the knowledge put her into a happier mood. Again she asked herself why she should care about his opinion of her. It didn't matter in the least.

At the same time she had no wish for a quarrel that would last the entire fortnight he would be with them, therefore she stepped closer to examine the work on his drawing-board. 'This is a floor plan?' she asked, looking at the lines that divided rooms.

'Most perceptive,' he drawled. 'Can you follow it?' He moved to stand beside her, then pointed to the various sections. 'There we have the three bedrooms. Bathroom and kitchen are within easy reach of each other because of the plumbing, and there is the lounge with a dinette attached to it. It should face north.'

She studied the plan in silence, conscious of his nearness and the tangy perfume of his aftershave, and that in some way his hand had come to rest upon her shoulder. Nor was it a light, impersonal touch, but a gentle rubbing of his thumb against her neck, his touch sending a quiver down her spine.

'I'm waiting to hear what you think,' he reminded her.

'The lounge would be improved by the addition of a north-west corner window,' she said, making an effort to keep her voice steady.

He frowned. 'What's wrong with that wide window across the front?'

She smiled. 'You've lived in sunny Queensland for too long. You've forgotten that in a New Zealand winter we need all the late afternoon sun we can get. A corner window gives it to us.'

Their heads drew closer together as they bent over the floor plan. His hand remained on her shoulder, the feather-light massaging of his thumb continuing to send tremors into her nerves, and while she knew the intimacy could be broken by simply moving away, she seemed unable to do so, until Estelle's icy tones came from the doorway.

'I trust I'm not interrupting anything. You did say ten o'clock.'

Rolf straightened his back. 'Yes. I think Kay's ready to begin.'

Estelle's eyes sent a green glow towards him. 'Do I look all right in this dress? I know it's only a head and shoulders.'

It was the same dress of green and gold shot silk she had worn the previous evening, and he now considered its low neck with the loose hair falling softly about her shoulders. 'You look beautiful, but then you always do.'

'Thank you, Rolf darling.' Her smile became brilliant as she flicked a look of veiled triumph towards Kay.

It had the effect of making Kay feel irritable, but she reminded herself that anger had no place in her mind at the moment. Besides, Rolf was right. Estelle did look quite beautiful. Then Kay pulled herself together and made an effort to take control of the situation by saying, 'Please sit in the model's chair, Estelle. I've raised you to nearer my eye level with the help of a cushion and bricks under each chair leg.'

Estelle went to the chair and settled herself into a comfortable position that enabled her to look into the studio. 'This is how I'll sit,' she decided, her voice indicating she did not intend to argue about it. 'I'll be able to watch Rolf working at his drawing-board.'

Kay smiled at her. 'I thought you'd like to do just that,' she said.

Estelle was surprised. 'You did? In that case you must realise that Rolf and I——' She broke off, her smile full of confidence.

Kay glanced towards the studio where Rolf was again busy at his board. If he had heard Estelle's words he gave no sign. Or had he deliberately ignored them? Then concentration took over as Kay picked up a stick of fine charcoal and began to place an outline on the canvas.

The oval she drew was placed with care. It was followed by the lines of a graceful neck, the droop of shoulders and folds of drapery forming the bodice of the dress. A few touches indicated the twirls of hair, and then she stood back to ascertain that the sketch had been suitably placed on the rectangle before her.

A start was then made on the face, and, beginning at the top of Estelle's nose, the charcoal searched for the bone structure between the eyes and the form of the brow. But even as Kay worked a smile spread over Estelle's face, while the glow in her eyes told Kay that Rolf had left his work to watch the procedure. 'Please hold the pose,' she requested, pausing with charcoal poised in her hand.

'Rolf knows that I always have a smile for him,' Estelle told her smugly, as though sure of her place in his affections.

Kay turned to look at him, and keeping her voice cool she said, 'Would you please return to your drawing-board so that the model can control her expression, otherwise I'll be unable to complete a satisfactory drawing.'

'Fair enough,' he commented.

'Thank you,' said Kay, ignoring the pout now marring Estelle's face.

Fifteen minutes later Kay put down her charcoal and said to Estelle, 'You may rest now. Leave the chair and move about.'

Estelle stood up and stretched herself. She gave only a cursory glance at the sketch, then went to the studio where she almost leaned against Rolf while watching him pencil the lines for the elevation of a side wall.

Watching them, Kay felt a further surge of impatience, this time its cause being fired by the easy familiarity that existed between Rolf and Estelle, but before her irritation could expand to any extent Ivy entered the lounge with a tray of steaming coffee mugs.

'Thank you, Ivy, you're a dear.' Kay took a mug from the tray, then moved to gaze unseeingly through the front window. Keeping her back towards Rolf and Estelle, she told herself she was being a fool. There was no need for their association to concern her, yet Estelle's proprietorial air towards this man seemed to do something to her. It got under her skin, needling her into a state of peevishness.

'I've been keeping an eye on the clock,' she heard Ivy say. 'I knew it was time for a break.'

'And time for Kay to rest her eyes,' Rolf's deep voice replied.

The comment caused Kay's brows to rise. It meant that his thoughts were not entirely centred upon Estelle, and the knowledge sent her back to the easel in a happier frame of mind.

As she settled down to work Rolf moved to stand beside her. 'Quite a respectable drawing,' he conceded, his tone holding guarded praise. 'I like the slight turn of the head and the angle of the shoulders, yet the eyes look at the viewer.'

'It's called the three-way pose—and the eyes will always follow whoever looks at the portrait. I'm glad you approve.'

Estelle said, 'Personally, I consider my eyes to be *much* larger.'

Kay ignored the remark by taking up a clean rag and applying a few light flicks that left only faint outlines. She then dipped a small brush in raw umber and proceeded to go over what remained of the lines, thus retaining the drawing as a more permanent guide. She knew that Rolf had returned to his drawing-board, and she noticed that Estelle was still standing beside her.

'You think you're very clever,' remarked Estelle with a veiled sneer. 'I'm telling you, this portrait had better be good or——'

Kay was taken aback by the open hostility, or was it jealousy of her ability? 'Yes? Or you'll do what?'

'I'll—I'll *burn* it.' The words were hissed quietly.

'Will it be yours to burn?'

Estelle tossed her head. 'I won't care who owns it.'

Kay refused to be riled. 'Then you'll have to help me make it a success by sitting perfectly still. Have you any preference for which expression goes on your face?'

Estelle sent her a look of suspicion. 'What do you mean by—expression?'

'Naturally you have a choice between the jealousy that appears to be simmering within you, and the superficial sweetness you offer to someone you wish to impress. No need to mention names.'

'You're having a joke at my expense,' Estelle accused her angrily. 'You'd better watch your tongue, as well as your brush strokes.'

Kay laughed. 'I think you mean my tone values, my lights and shadows which are the secret of expression.'

Estelle glared at her, then flounced back to the model's chair.

The work continued with Kay mixing dark flesh tones which were laid in the shadowed areas while the light caused them to be plainly visible. By the time the next break came they formed a series of dark blotches outlining the side of Estelle's face and jaw. They lay beneath her nose, lower lip and chin, on the shaded side of her neck and in the vicinity of her eyes.

Estelle took one horrified look, then whirled into the studio where she complained in a loud voice, 'She's making me look like a clown, and if you think I'm putting up with this sort of thing——'

Rolf came to view the work. 'I see nothing wrong with it,' he said after a pause.

Estelle was aghast. 'You *don't*? You see nothing wrong with all that mess on my face?'

'Don't be stupid, Stell. One usually starts with the darks when working with oils.'

Kay looked at him with interest. 'You've been holding back on me. I believe you know more about painting than you've admitted.'

'Well, yes, it was my love of sketching buildings that caused me to turn to architecture. Some day I intend to take it up again, when I can find the time, and perhaps someone to sketch with me.'

His words caused Kay's pulses to quicken. It would be pleasant to go out painting with Rolf, she thought wistfully. They would work on the same scene, helping each other with suggestions about composition, and discussing which colours to use. They would have a packed lunch, and after a day of amiable companionship they would come home with sketches to be completed in the studio. And then Estelle's voice cut into her dreaming.

'Rolf dear, are you saying you'd like me to learn to paint? I'm sure Kay would teach me, that's if *you* ask her.'

Kay held her breath as she awaited his answer.

'Of course, I'd *pay* her to teach me,' Estelle went on as though fully confident that Kay couldn't possibly refuse.

Rolf looked at her with tolerance. 'I believe you'd derive much pleasure from painting.'

'Of course I would,' said Estelle with enthusiasm. 'Mother says I'm so *creative*, so very *artistic*, so please arrange with her to teach me.' The last words came pleadingly, then she added, 'It can't be so very difficult. I mean, if *Kay* can do it, I'm sure that I could do it a whole lot——' She had the grace to fall silent.

'*Better?*' Kay finished for her. She then turned to Rolf, waiting for him to begin the campaign of asking her to teach Estelle to paint. Just let him utter one plea, she thought fiercely. He'll get a brushload of titanium white right in the eye.

Perhaps her feelings conveyed themselves to him, because he merely shrugged and said to Estelle, 'Isn't it time you were back in the chair? The session will end at noon.'

'But you haven't asked her,' Estelle protested.

'Nor shall I do so,' he retorted firmly. 'It is for you to make your own arrangements.' And with those terse words he strode back into the studio and closed the door.

The rest of the sitting went smoothly, but without further mention of painting lessons, and by the time it ended at midday Kay had made progress by surrounding Estelle's head and shoulders with a grey-green background. And although the model's expression had become sulky, this did not find its way to the canvas.

However, when twelve o'clock came Estelle did not appear to be anxious to leave, and in what could only be considered a blatant angling for an invitation she smiled sweetly at Ivy and said, 'Mother is not really expecting me home for lunch. She won't mind if I stay.'

But Ivy equalled her guile by returning with matching

sweetness, 'Well now, won't it be a pleasant surprise for her when you walk in the door. Goodbye, Estelle, we'll see you next Saturday. Same time, same dress, same hairstyle, remember.'

'Yes, well—goodbye,' Estelle muttered with a last glance at the closed studio door before taking a reluctant leave.

Her departure filled Kay with relief. Never before had she felt a model's antagonism towards her, and the experience was not a pleasant one. It filled her with dismay, but she assured herself she would overcome it. By the time the portrait was finished she would have ceased to allow Estelle's barbed remarks to upset her.

Nor must her own feelings, caused by this state of affairs, be reflected in her work. The finished portrait must show a clean, vibrant result, depicting the happy personality Estelle imagined herself to portray. And no doubt this aspect of her nature was presented to the world when things went her way, although Kay had a strong suspicion that Estelle's underlying bitchiness indicated that things were not going her way.

For that matter, things were not going very well in Kay's direction, and as soon as lunch was finished she returned to the portrait, mainly as a means of combating the depression building steadily in her mind.

Rolf came to stand beside her. 'I understood that painting without the model was against the rule.'

She paused, brush in hand. 'As you can see, I'm not touching the face, but the folds in the dress have already been sketched in, and the colour tones for them have been mixed. I didn't get round to putting them on earlier, nor do I intend to waste this paint.'

'How long do you intend to work?'

'Until this dress paint is used, and then I'll clean my brushes and palette.' She glanced up to find his eyes examining her hair, and from its golden lights their gaze held hers until she became aware of a slow flush rising towards her cheeks. In an effort to remain calm she asked casually, 'How do you intend to spend your afternoon?'

'I'll work in the studio until you've finished your brush and palette-cleaning chore, then I'll take you out for a breath of fresh air. We'll drive to Napier.'

Her brown eyes held a surprised question. 'You're so sure I'll come with you?'

'Of course you'll come. Why shouldn't you?'

'It's possible I have no wish to—to be with one who considers I'm full of low cunning. The old sympathy trick you accused me of playing, remember?' It was difficult to keep the tremor from her voice, or to smother the hurt which rose as she recalled his words of the previous evening.

'You're not thinking straight,' he told her bluntly. 'Your concentration on that portrait has made you feel tired. Just slap on the paint and call it a day.'

'I *never* just slap on the paint,' she declared indignantly. 'I try to make every brush stroke a statement of what I can see before me. This is not an abstract, you know.'

'Of course I'm aware of that fact, and I also know that you're taking everything too seriously, especially anything I may have said last night.'

'*Really*?' Her voice became icy. 'Then let me tell you that a slur on my character is not something that amuses me. To me it is serious,' she admitted, her expression bleak as she turned away from him, conscious of a sudden prickling behind her eyelids.

He became impatient. 'OK, OK, if you don't wish to drive to Napier with me, just forget it. I merely thought you looked tired and would enjoy an outing in the fresh air.'

And then she knew a sense of irritation as the brush became unsteady in her hand, causing her to put a light tone in the shadow of the fold where it should have remained dark. '*Blast*!' she exclaimed, picking up her palette knife to scrape it off.

'I said you were tired,' he jeered.

Suddenly she knew she was taking a stupid attitude. He was inviting her to drive to Napier in that smart Porsche, and she hadn't the sense to accept gracefully. Somewhat contritely she admitted, 'You're right. I am tired. It's because I haven't worked on a portrait for ages and the concentration has been more intense than usual. Yes, please, I'd like to come.'

He looked at her critically then grinned. 'It's nice to see a girl who can get off a high horse before it bucks. Personally, I'd say the intense concentration has knocked you flat. OK, I'll be ready when you are.'

She resisted the urge to tell him that part of her weariness had been caused by the model's attitude towards her. However, his concern lifted her spirits, and she set to work on the dress folds with renewed vigour.

Instead of returning to the studio he stood watching as she continued to place the darkest hues along the inner folds, then graded the tones until the lightest areas were reached. 'You seem to know what you're doing,' he conceded with almost grudging admiration. 'One can positively see the rounded turn of the material.'

He was right. Her efforts had resulted in a three-dimensional effect, with the cloth catching the light coming through the end window of the lounge, and secretly she revelled in being able to display her ability to this man. 'It's all a matter of having the know-how,' she told him nonchalantly.

Little more than an hour later she was sitting beside him in the Porsche, and as a feeling of quiet contentment began to steal over her she pushed it aside, just as she had closed her mind to Ivy's comment when she had come downstairs.

'You look nice,' the older woman had whispered, her grey eyes moving over Kay's teal-blue sundress and matching jacket. 'I'm glad he's asked you to go out. I know you'll enjoy yourself.'

Kay had smiled and kissed her. 'You're saying that only because he reminds you of somebody. But you must remember, he's not Arnold.'

But these thoughts slid from her mind as the car drew near the corner shop where it stopped before turning on to the main road. Then, just as it was about to continue, someone emerged from the shop, and there was no mistaking the slim figure of Estelle.

She stood still, taking in the sight of Kay in the passenger seat before she shrieked, 'Rolf, Rolf!'

He hesitated for the briefest moment before moving the car on to the grassy verge, then, muttering words that Kay was unable to catch, leapt from the vehicle and strode across the road to speak to Estelle.

Kay sat and watched, conscious of a rising irritation. Estelle has only to raise her voice and he runs to her side, she thought with impatience, and as she saw a smile break over the redhead's face she knew that Rolf's explanation of her presence in the car was giving satisfaction. Curiosity then gripped her. What exactly was he saying to placate Estelle?

But when Rolf returned to the car he gave no indication of the conversation which had caused Estelle's expression to change. Instead, he merely stared straight ahead as they drove through the cultivated areas between Te Awanga and the township of Clive where they turned on to the Napier highway.

At last she could bear the silence no longer, therefore she said, 'You're very quiet. Is something wrong?'

He grinned at her. 'What could be wrong?'

'I've no idea, but I'm wondering if perhaps you were wishing that Estelle was sitting beside you instead of me.'

'Don't be silly.'

'I'd have quite understood if you'd——'

'If I'd told you to get out at the corner shop and walk home?'

'It wouldn't have been far,' she pointed out. 'It was only a short distance along the road.

His tone became impatient. 'Just get this straight. If I'd wanted Estelle to be sitting in that seat she'd have been there. Have you got that clear in your mind?'

She nodded, conscious of a sense of satisfaction, then, still probing, she said, 'Well, Estelle didn't seem to mind too much. I mean about me sitting in her seat. She was smiling happily when you left her.'

'Really?'

'Surely you noticed? She has a lovely smile.'

He made no reply and she knew he was not to be drawn in the matter of Estelle. At the same time she couldn't help wondering why the sight of her in Rolf's car had not brought forth a tantrum rather than a smile, and suspicion began to niggle at Kay. There was something wrong somewhere, but at the moment she was unable to put her finger on it.

CHAPTER SIX

KAY pondered the question while the car glided across the bridges of the three rivers which brought so much shingle down from the ranges, and as they turned on to the long straight seafront road leading to the Parade she said, 'You have a special reason for coming to Napier this afternoon?'

'A couple of reasons,' Rolf admitted. 'The first was to give you an outing.'

She turned to him gratefully, her brown eyes shining. 'Thank you, you're very kind. And the second reason?'

'I need to collect an extra block of drawing-paper, as well as a roll of newsprint for sketches of preliminary ideas for plans. It doesn't matter when I'm working at the office because there's always plenty to hand, but such is not the case when I'm working at home or elsewhere.'

'Do you often work away from the office?'

'I've been known to sit on a building-site and sketch the house I think should be constructed to go there.'

Leaving the Parade, with its rows of sheltering Norfolk pines, he drove to an area where office blocks seemed to predominate. Among them was a long modern building with an opulent front door, and as he parked beside it he sent her an affable grin. 'Would you be interested in seeing my office?'

She had no wish to sound eager, but found difficulty in keeping the hint of excitement from her voice as she said, 'Yes, please.'

The surge of pleasure was still with her as he ushered her through the door. She was about to see where he worked, and in some vague way it gave her a feeling of intimacy with this man whose mere presence seemed to stir an inner excitement.

His office was at the end of the passage, and as they passed closed doors on either side their feet made no sound on the carpet's thick pile. He stood aside for her to enter the room, and moments later she had become intrigued by the sight of large drawing-boards resting upon stands, each with a small lamp attached to its top, plus 'straight-edge' mechanism to give parallel motion up and down the board.

And, while he collected the paper he needed, she examined the array of technical-drawing instruments until suddenly she became aware that he was standing beside her. His closeness caused her to take a sharp breath, but if he noticed it he ignored it.

'You're interested in set-squares and T-squares?' he drawled, then pointed to an object incorporating a curved edge. 'That particular toy is a technograph. It's a combination of a set-square and a protractor for laying out or measuring angles.'

She stepped away from him, wondering why his nearness caused her pulses to leap. 'I'm afraid my technical tools are very meagre,' she admitted, managing to keep the slight tremor from her voice. 'Apart from a set-square, all I possess is a ruler to help with perspective when sketching an old barn.'

He examined the collection on the bench. 'If there's anything you'd like to have, it's yours.'

His generosity caused her to feel a rush of warm gratitude. Ivy was right, she thought. He was like Arnold—kind and generous. However, she said, 'Oh, no, thank you, I don't need anything more for the work I do. I'll just stay with the gannets and—and small scenes.'

'And the occasional portrait?'

'I'll admit it's what I like doing most of all. It's a challenge.'

'Especially when you have a beautiful model.'

'Yes, especially then.' His words had acted like a dash

of icy water. They had taken the pleasure from the moment, making her feel dull and depressed, although she forced herself to ask lightly, 'Have you collected sufficient paper?'

'I hope so. In any case I can always come back for more.' He paused, regarding her thoughtfully. 'How would you feel about a walk along the Parade?'

'That would be pleasant.' Somehow her earlier feeling of intimacy had disappeared, and she knew it had been swept away by his reference to a beautiful model. It meant, of course, that despite her presence Estelle was uppermost in his mind.

He sent her a sharp look. 'Do I detect a lack of enthusiasm?'

She made a hasty denial. 'Not at all. I love the Parade with its bright gardens, its fountain and all the entertainment it provides for every age-group. And Pania of the Reef, that bronze statue of a Maori girl, just fascinates me.'

'You've painted her, I suppose?'

'Yes, several times, but they've all been sold.'

'Then let's go and talk to her. She might offer advice.'

Her brows rose. 'You consider we need advice?'

'Everyone needs advice, sooner or later.'

She laughed. 'I'm not sure I'd take Pania's advice. She wasn't very wise.'

The paper was stored in the Porsche, then they drove to the Parade where a parking-place was found near the life-sized statue of a Maori girl sitting on a rock. The figure had been expertly sculptured to capture the smooth roundness of legs, arms and breasts, while the beautiful face held a look of serenity as she gazed out to sea.

The Maori legend told how Pania, lured by the siren voices of the sea people, swam out to meet them. But when she tried to return to her lover she was transformed into the reef which lies beyond the Napier breakwater.

Kay read the words aloud.

Rolf listened then said with a grin, 'Let that be a lesson to you.'

The remark surprised her. 'Lesson? What do you mean?'

'Don't run away from your lover. Stay close to his side.'

She became indignant. 'I haven't a lover, nor am I likely to become involved with one.'

He made no reply as he led her along the flower-bordered path towards the sound shell, and then beyond it to where players were busy on the putting green. Leaning on a rail to watch balls roll along the miniature greens, he asked casually, 'Would you say no to a cup of tea?'

'Indeed I would not, but where do we find one, when most places are closed for a Saturday afternoon holiday?'

'I know where the kettle can be boiled and a biscuit produced.'

They returned to the car and he drove along the road that led out of Napier until an opening enabled him to turn beneath the centre line of pines. He then drove back beside the houses on the inward road, and moments later turned through an opening which led to the back of a modern block of flats.

The area held a car park with garages below the upper floor, and as he led her up a stairway to a balcony she looked about her then asked, 'There's a tearoom here?'

'Not exactly, but we can at least make a cup of tea for ourselves.'

It was then she realised he had brought her to his flat.

The door he unlocked led into a well-furnished living-room that extended across the apartment to windows giving views of the Parade and its activities. A kitchen opened from it, and she could also see into a short passage which appeared to give access to three bedrooms and a bathroom.

'You're welcome to look round while I make the tea,' he invited. 'You might even like to wash your hands in the bathroom. You'll find clean hand towels in the small wall cupboard.'

'Thank you.' Again she appreciated his thoughtfulness.

She used the bathroom and then curiosity took control, urging her to peep into the three bedrooms. They were larger than she had expected, and surprisingly orderly. The smallest served as a guest-room, while the second had been converted into a workroom. She then stood hesitating before entering the largest of the bedrooms, mainly because of the sudden realisation that it was *his* room, and because she was assailed by the feeling that she was spying.

The amused tones of his voice came from behind her. 'You're allowed to go in—or are you feeling timid about entering a man's room?'

She turned to find him regarding her from the living-room doorway, his intensely blue eyes full of amusement as he observed her hesitation.

'Why should I feel timid?' she challenged him, then walked boldly into the room. But almost immediately she wanted to leave it because it held an aura of maleness that was somehow disturbing. Or was it because it had become stamped with Rolf Warburton's personality?

His accessories on the dressing-table, his clothes visible through the half-open wardrobe door, even the pile of *Good Homes* magazines on the bedside table, helped to bring back the previous feeling of intimacy, and she found herself filled with an unexpected desire to straighten the cover of the casually made bed. However, she resisted the impulse and moved to the window which also overlooked the Parade, and through the Norfolk pine branches towards the sea.

He followed her into the room. 'Tea's made—or would you rather be tossed on to the bed?'

She gave a nervous laugh. 'I'd prefer the tea, thank you.'

'You're lying and you know it. You've got hot blood swirling beneath that cool exterior.' His eyes held a strange intensity.

She spoke lightly. 'You consider yourself to be an authority on the temperature of my blood?'

'I can feel the warmth you're so intent upon keeping hidden. I doubt that you've ever had a passionate affair.'

She became indignant. 'Really, you make me sound like a poor pathetic twit—a neglected ninny . . .'

'That was not my intention.' He moved to draw her away from the window, then his hands on her shoulders turned her to face him. 'I'm trying to say that I feel you are still—untouched. You've never—known man, as the saying goes. Emotionally you're still soundly sleeping, waiting to be awakened. To cut a long story short, you're still a virgin. True?'

She nodded, looking at him wordlessly as the colour flooded into her face. His grip on her shoulders sent a tremor through her body and her pulses began to pound as his arms moved to hold her against the long length of his form.

She closed her eyes, leaning against his shoulder, and as he rested his cheek on her forehead his fingers became entwined in her hair. The silence between them filled her with an inner peace, but this was short-lived, because when his lips found hers she became conscious of a glow that spread through her senses, sweeping her mind into a bemused state.

She also knew that his hand had moved from her hair to cup her breast, his thumb gently caressing her raised nipple. The action sent waves of delicious pleasure through her entire being, waves that heightened as his hand crept slowly down her spine, massaging its way with sensuous expertise until it reached and gripped her buttock.

The pressure against his body made her more than aware of his arousal, and she knew that his passion called for her response. Nor had she any control over the intensity of the rapturous sensations that sent her nerves curling into flames of desire.

His deepening kiss caused her to respond with more ecstasy than she realised, and suddenly he paused to murmur with satisfaction, 'Ah, not so cold, after all?'

Unable to find words, she was also unaware of the light glowing in her eyes, a light that betrayed her deep longing to surrender to his lovemaking, and recognising it he murmured softly, 'I can fix it, you know.'

She looked at him in a dazed manner. 'Fix it?'

'That virginity. The double bed is there, waiting—and I'd be gentle.'

His words brought her down to earth. She gulped, then became conscious of a slight trembling which caused her to step back from him. He could speak of her virginity so *lightly*?

His eyes narrowed as he surveyed her state of nervousness. 'Or perhaps you'd prefer to have that cup of tea.'

She grasped at the suggestion. 'Yes, please, I'd rather have the tea—if you don't mind.'

His mouth twisted into a grim smile. 'OK. I'll see if I can find a cup with anticlimax written on it.' Then, leaving her abruptly, he strode towards the kitchen.

She remained in the bedroom for several minutes before finding the courage to follow him, and when she reached the living-room she found he had already poured the tea.

They drank it while sitting at the table near the

window, and, because of the painful shyness that now gripped her, Kay found difficulty in meeting Rolf's eyes. She knew he was watching her with veiled amusement, but she kept her head turned from him while making a pretence of studying the people who walked below on the other side of the road.

'More tea?' he asked, refilling her cup, then added gravely, 'There now, that should help to wash away all that embarrassment. I know it's really bugging you.'

She turned accusing eyes upon him. 'I know you're laughing at me—I know you think I'm an idiot.'

He refilled his own cup. 'Do you care what I think?'

She considered the question and found she had to be honest. 'Yes, I suppose I do.'

He regarded her intently. 'Strange as it seems, I care about your opinion of me. I wouldn't like you to imagine I'd brought you here with an ulterior motive.'

'Is that what you call it? I thought it was just a matter of male necessity—something to be tasted and then tossed aside.'

'Naturally you find that difficult to understand.'

She became indignant. 'Of course I do. I'm afraid a casual encounter has no appeal for me. It leaves me cold. I need——' She fell silent as the word trailed away.

'Yes? What do you need?' The question came softly.

'I need——' She hesitated, staring into her cup before going on quietly, 'I need substance, rather than a brief experience.'

'You're saying you need love to go along with your lovemaking.'

'That's right. And we both know that you don't love me. You love Estelle, but you refuse to admit it, even to yourself.' She had a vision of Estelle smiling at him outside the corner shop, and again she wondered what reason he had given for her own presence in his car.

He gave a short laugh. 'It's obvious you know nothing about the direction of my affections.'

She made no reply, waiting for a denial that his affections involved Estelle, but it did not come. And then another recollection struck her, one that caused her to change the subject. 'Didn't you say the noise of the children and cars would be distracting to your work? I can see lots of children, yet their shouting doesn't seem to reach here.'

'Actually, we're above the noise unless there's an easterly wind to blow it this way.'

'And the cars have slowed down because they're in a built-up area, therefore the noise that would disturb you isn't so bad after all.'

'So what are you trying to fathom, Madam Detective?'

'So why come to Te Awanga? It can't have been for the sea air because you've already got it here—although it would give you a period near Estelle.'

'And her mother,' he added drily. 'Mrs Lexington-Barron might be a managing Juno, but I haven't forgotten she was always very kind to me when I was a boy.'

Kay smiled. 'Why Juno?'

'Because Juno considered herself to be queen of heaven.'

Kay cut in, 'Wasn't she also the patroness of marriage?'

He ignored the interruption. 'She was said to have been both wife and sister of Jupiter, but I'm afraid the late Mr Barron was a far cry from Jupiter.'

'I've heard very little about him. I mean Mr Barron, not Jupiter.'

'He died years ago, a thin, aesthetic man who suffered indifferent health. His wife nursed him until the end.'

Kay said, 'I can understand her desire to have Estelle living near by when she's married.'

'Desire? Don't you mean her determination?'

'Well, I doubt that she'll have to fight hard,' then, hastily, 'In what way was she kind when you were a boy?'

'Oh, she always made me welcome by asking me to tea and so forth. And once she arranged a surprise party for my birthday, but it wasn't a surprise because Estelle whispered in my ear, telling me about all the preparations that were going on.'

'Wasn't that rather mean of her?'

He shrugged. 'She was so excited she couldn't keep her mouth shut.'

'That's right, make excuses for her,' said Kay, hoping she didn't sound as cross as she felt, then, making an effort to leave the subject of Estelle and her mother, she looked about the living-room and said, 'It's really a lovely flat. Everything is so new.'

'The block was planned by our firm, so I had the advantage of being able to buy the one I wanted. You haven't examined the kitchen. It leaves little to be desired in culinary requirements.'

They left the table and she followed him to the kitchen where he indicated its modern design and conveniences. And from there he led her through the flat, pointing out other neat house-planning ideas she had missed during her first survey.

At last he said with a hint of satisfaction, 'I think it has everything anyone could wish for.'

'I haven't noticed a laundry,' her practical mind forced her to say. 'Where does one wash clothes?'

'Downstairs. There's a washing machine as well as a clothes drier in the garage. Soiled linen goes down a chute from the bathroom. Anything else?' His raised brows emphasised the question.

She hesitated, then admitted, 'I can't help wondering about struggling up and down those outside stairs when it's wet and windy.'

'There's no need to use them. When I arrive home on

a dirty wet night an electronic hand device in the car opens and closes the garage door. I drive in without getting out of the car, and then I go up on an inner staircase. Come, I'll show you.'

He led her back to the lounge, then crossed the room to a door set in the end wall. She had noticed it previously but had presumed it to be a cupboard, and he now opened it to reveal a narrow flight of steps. A light was switched on to illuminate the way down to the garage where there were shelves and cupboards for storage, as well as the laundry appliances.

He waved an arm at the latter. 'You see, all mod cons. And if you prefer to hang clothes in the sun, rather than use the drier, there are lines at the end of the parking-yard. Do you think that Ivy would——' He paused as though deciding against uttering the question he was about to ask.

She turned to look at him, suddenly aware of a vague uneasiness. 'Yes? Do I think that Ivy would what?'

'Well, would she approve of a place such as this?'

Her unease grew into apprehension as she said carefully, 'I'm sure she'd consider it to be a most convenient flat.'

He frowned, betraying an underlying impatience. 'What I'm trying to say is, do you think she'd be comfortable living in it?'

She felt a chill creeping over her as the meaning behind his words began to register, but she forced her voice to remain casual as she said, 'Comfortable? I really don't know. You see, Ivy is accustomed to having space about her, and where space is concerned one cannot compare a flat with a house—especially with a house that has the presence of a man one loved still hovering about the rooms.'

He gave a snort of derision. 'Personally, I think she's being quite ridiculous. One can't live with the dead, and that's exactly what Ivy is doing. Nor do I consider you're doing anything to help the situation. In fact, I doubt that you can even see it clearly.'

His attack caused her jaw to sag slightly, and, gaping at him she almost quavered, 'What can I do——'

'You can help drag her mind out of Arnold's grave,' he rasped. 'You can make an attempt to get her back to normal, but for this to happen she must be prised out of that house.'

She became indignant. 'I do not find Ivy to be abnormal.'

'That's because you're so busy in your studio, wrapped up in doing your own thing. And what's more, you've become so used to Ivy she doesn't strike you as being odd.'

'Of course she doesn't, because she's not *odd*. She's merely grieving.' Kay's loyalty rose to the top.

'Then let me tell you that her constant talk about Arnold strikes me all the time. I do wonder if she isn't slightly unbalanced. I'm amazed you can't see it for yourself.'

'How dare you speak to me in this manner? I won't listen to another word you have to say.' She turned and ran up the stairs to the living-room, then almost raced across to the windows, where she stared unseeingly at the stiffly extended branches of the Norfolk pines. And as she considered the situation the chill that had previously gripped her began to intensify as various points cleared themselves in her mind.

She also knew he had followed and was now standing behind her, and when she spoke the calmness of her own voice surprised her. 'Now I know why I was offered this—this *pleasant* outing.'

'You mean you *think* you know. Perhaps you could share these—suppositions. I'm all ears, so let's have them.'

She faced him angrily. 'Very well. To begin with, your main purpose in bringing me to Napier was to show me this flat. Oh yes, I know you said you needed extra paper, but that was merely the excuse you used.'

A shade of annoyance crossed his face. 'Is that a fact? Why should I wish to show you this flat?' he demanded coldly.

'To win my approval of it as a future residence for Ivy.' Even as she uttered the words the picture became clearer. 'It's possible your plan is to make an exchange, but I'm afraid this flat would be too expensive for Ivy.'

'You're forgetting that its cost would be taken care of by the trustees. It would be the same as the house——'

'Then I'm right. You did have an exchange in mind. Therefore all that—that affection you showered upon me in the bedroom didn't mean a thing. It was merely an attempt to soften me, to move me towards your way of thinking when the subject of making an exchange is brought forward.' She began to fume inwardly. 'And *you* dared to accuse *me* of subterfuge. The old sympathy trick, you said. *Huh*!'

His mouth tightened as his jaw hardened. Blue sparks glittered from between narrowed lids. 'Have you any further deductions, Madam Detective?' The words came as a snarl.

'Only that you were determined to use me to persuade Ivy to comply with your plans. And naturally those plans include Estelle.' She stopped, biting her lip and furious with herself for having uttered those last words.

'Estelle? You're so sure about that?' he drawled in a tone of derision.

'How can I be otherwise? That smile on her face as you left her at the corner shop now speaks for itself. At first I was puzzled by it—but now it is more than obvious that you explained why I was in your car and what you had in mind. She'll be agog to know how successful you've been.'

'You've got it all wrong,' he snapped furiously.

'I think not. Now shall we go home? I'm sorry your

mission has failed, but it's nothing to the manner in which this entire outing has failed as—as far as I'm concerned.'

A sudden gush of tears filled her eyes. She brushed them away angrily, and, hoping he hadn't seen them, she turned swiftly towards the door. Rapid steps took her down the outside stairway to where the car stood parked beside the garage door, and, getting into it, she sat waiting until he had checked and locked the flat.

The drive towards home was made almost in silence; nevertheless there were moments when she took sly peeps at the dark scowl on his brow, the sight of it being enough to discourage her from trying to converse.

However, a stop was made as they drew near to Te Awanga. A noticeboard outside the entrance to a commercial grower's property caught Rolf's eye and, reducing speed, he turned into a long avenue of apple trees where laden branches were bowed beneath the weight of ripening fruit.

A stall at the end of the drive enabled Rolf to make purchases of lettuces, tomatoes, cucumbers and other vegetables, and as Kay helped to store the bags of produce in the car she said, 'You seem to have bought an awful lot.' At the same time she was glad of a reason to break the icy wall that had risen between them.

'Ivy does not have to bear the expense of the food I eat,' he said gruffly. 'On Monday I'll take you to the corner shop, and if you'll fill her grocery cupboard I'll be most grateful.'

When they reached home they found Ivy in a happy mood, which became even more cheerful as she surveyed the fruit and vegetables. As she stored them away she uttered a deep sigh. 'Ah, those lovely long telegraph cucumbers. Arnold loved cucumber and tomato sandwiches with my home-made salad dressing. Thank you so much.' She smiled at Rolf, then added, 'I've put some of Arnold's magazines on your bedside

table. I felt sure you'd be interested in them. And we're
having Arnold's favourite casserole for dinner . . .'

Kay gave a quiet chuckle. 'You can't win,' she
whispered to Rolf, then hurried upstairs to her room.

The following week passed with surprising speed,
perhaps because it proved to be extra busy. It began on
Monday with a trip to the corner shop, where Rolf
insisted upon Kay choosing every commodity that Ivy
could need, plus numerous items of food for the deep
freeze.

The car appeared to be laden, and as they drove home
she said, 'I thought you were trying to get us out of
Hope House, but from the look of this lot anyone
would imagine we were preparing for a siege.'

He made no reply.

She went on, 'Nor am I sure how she'll take to bought
pies. She always makes her own—the sort that Arnold
liked,' she added with a sly peep in his direction.

'Then she can feed them to the workmen tomorrow.
Knowing Ivy, I'm sure she'll insist upon giving them
lunch.'

The words surprised her, causing her to turn to him
with a puzzled air. 'Workmen?'

'The dishwasher. It'll arrive tomorrow, brought by a
couple of men who will install it.'

'Oh. Estelle will be delighted.'

'What has it to do with Estelle?' he queried in cool
tones.

'Well, we both know who will be using it eventually.'
She swallowed to ease her throat, which seemed to have
become suddenly constricted as she chided herself in
silent reproach. Why, oh, why had it been necessary to
utter those words?

'Does your certainty that Estelle will be using it mean
you've decided to talk to Ivy about the flat?' he asked
lightly, his voice holding a teasing note.

'Definitely not,' she flashed, betraying her irritation. 'The housing situation is entirely between Ivy and you. It has nothing to do with me. I refuse to interfere.'

'You needn't be afraid of losing your studio. That third bedroom makes an excellent workroom.'

'No doubt.' She closed her lips firmly, refusing to discuss the matter further, mainly because she felt hurt by something she was unable to define. Perhaps its roots lay in the fact that he could hold her so closely, kiss her with such mad fever—yet be contemplating marriage with Estelle.

Her greatest need, she realised, was control over her own wayward emotions. She must force her mind into a state of casual indifference towards him, but in this she was only partly successful because, no matter how hard she tried, she found herself longing for his kiss.

During the week their relationship merged into a state of easy companionship which found them laughing together over trifling incidents. When the tide was high they swam in the sea, on a few occasions persuading Ivy to paddle near by. But when they swam alone Kay found difficulty in keeping her eyes from Rolf's broad shoulders, his flat stomach and narrow hips. His long legs were well-shaped, and the crisp, dark hairs on his chest drew her attention with an irresistible force, while her longing to touch them became quite absurd.

However, he made no further attempts to kiss her, and this threw her into a state of discontent. While one half of her mind stated this to be a relief, the other half seethed with yearning to feel his arms about her. At the same time she recognised this to be a truth she had no intention of facing, therefore she pushed it away and concentrated upon work in the studio.

Nor did she allow Rolf's presence to distract her attention, although she was fully aware that he worked at his drawing-board. From the corner of her eye she watched him making measurements, ruling lines,

crumpling discarded paper into balls which he threw
into the waste-paper basket, sometimes with muttered
oaths.

One one occasion she said, 'Rolf, does the fact that
I'm here disturb you? I mean, I can easily work
elsewhere.'

He looked at her long and intently before answering,
causing her to wonder if she had made a stupid
suggestion until he said, 'Not at all. In any case I'm
about to drop this job and crawl under the house with a
strong light.'

'For Pete's sake, whatever for?'

'To search for borer. I understand the house is built
of heart timber, but I'd like to check the floorboards
and joists.'

He left her to work alone and it was then she realised
just how lonely she felt without him. Blast him, she
muttered to herself. He distracts me when he's here, and
he disturbs me when he's not here. It was something she
knew she must learn to combat.

By the time Saturday came she had three small gannet
studies to show for her pains, while progress had also
been made on the portrait's background and drapery of
the model's dress.

Estelle, who arrived at ten o'clock, examined the
latter critically, then conceded, 'You've got the colour
perfectly, but of course it's my face that's so
important—my clear complexion . . .'

'I'll do my best,' Kay smiled, amused by the other's
vanity.

Estelle noted the studio's emptiness. 'Where's Rolf?'
she asked peevishly. 'He knew I'd be coming this
morning.'

Ivy, who had opened the door to her, explained,
'He's up in the ceiling. He carried a ladder up the stairs
and has gone in through a trapdoor above the linen
cupboard. During the week he's been giving the house a

thorough examination, searching for patches of damp
or borer. I told him that Arnold had already had it
examined, but he said he wanted to check it for
himself.'

'He likes everything to be perfect. Well, almost,'
Estelle said with a complacent smile, then she turned to
Kay. 'Have you told Ivy about his flat?'

Kay became wary. 'His flat?'

'Yes. When he took you to Napier last Saturday I
suggested he should take you to see his flat.'

Kay stared at her. '*You* suggested——?'

Estelle became impatient. 'Yes. He spoke to me
outside the shop, remember? He said he needed to
collect extra paper and I thought it would be a good
opportunity for you to be shown his flat, and then you
could tell Ivy what an excellent place it would be to
move into.'

Ivy broke in. 'What's all this about moving?'

Estelle smiled sweetly. 'I think Kay knows what I'm
talking about.'

Ivy turned to Kay, her eyes alive with interest. 'You
didn't tell me you'd been to Rolf's flat.'

'It's got everything one could wish for,' Estelle
enthused, then went on to describe the modern
attributes of the flat.

Kay listened in silence, knowing that her reasons for
not mentioning the flat might be difficult to explain. If
she herself had jumped to the conclusion that Rolf had
an exchange of residential quarters in mind, wouldn't it
be possible that Ivy could do the same?

But Rolf's presence in the house had brought much
joy to Ivy, and Kay had no wish to say anything that
would switch it into a disappointment. This would
surely happen if Ivy began to suspect Rolf's motives for
showing her through his flat.

And then she felt a twinge of guilt as she recalled
accusing Rolf of the plan she now realised had come

from Estelle. What a fool she had been. If she had stopped to think about it she might have guessed its origin.

But at the moment she had no intention of allowing these irritating recollections to interfere with her concentration on the task in hand, and it became easier to brush them aside as she buttoned the front of her painting-smock. Then, squeezing daubs of paint across the outer curve of her clean palette, she took up a pliable knife and began to mix different grades of skin tones.

For the next sitting-period there was almost complete silence while the image of Estelle continued to evolve on the canvas. The model, it seemed, had no wish for conversation, but this did not worry Kay because it enabled her to pay full attention to the building up of form, the modelling of forehead, cheekbones and chin.

Ivy, who had been keeping an eye on the clock, arrived with coffee during the second rest-period, and she was soon followed by Rolf, to whom she had given a call. Estelle brightened at the sight of him, and Kay knew that her own cheeks felt slightly warmer. It would be safer to ignore him, she decided.

He was in a slightly dishevelled state, his thick, dark hair tumbling across his forehead, his navy cotton shirt sprinkled with dust and draped with cobwebs. Yet despite this unkempt state he still managed to look magnificent.

Ivy became motherly. She began picking long grey strands of web from his shoulders, giving a slight shudder as she confessed, 'I loathe cobwebs and spiders. Nasty creepy-crawly things. I hope you haven't brought any down with you.'

Rolf gave a deep throaty chuckle. 'I doubt it, and there's no need for you to go clambering up there with a spray can.'

Estelle spoke scornfully. 'Are you saying you're

actually afraid of spiders, Ivy?'

'Absolutely terrified of them,' the older woman admitted cheerfully. 'Now then, do you mind if we stop talking about them? Rolf, you haven't said what you think of the portrait. I've noticed you looking at it.'

He spoke gravely. 'I'm afraid to give Kay too much praise in case it goes to her head. To be honest, I think it's coming along in fine style and that she's very clever.'

Kay turned to look at him, searching for sincerity in his face and then feeling satisfied with what she saw. It made her glow inwardly and gave her the confidence she needed.

However, praise of Kay's ability was not appreciated by Estelle. 'You two appear to have forgotten that *I'm* the one who must approve of this portrait,' she exclaimed crossly. 'I don't care how—how brilliant you consider Kay to be—if I don't like it I won't accept it, and that's flat.'

Rolf sent her an easy grin. 'Who said you're the one who'll be accepting it?' he queried.

Estelle's expression changed. '*Of course*, you're having it done for *yourself*. How could I forget that important fact? OK, I'll behave. I'll sit still.'

She settled herself into her pose, and for the remainder of the session the expression on her face was almost angelic. It told Kay that her thoughts were with Rolf—but were his thoughts with Estelle? Wasn't the portrait enough to tell her that they were?

CHAPTER SEVEN

IVY gathered the coffee mugs and placed them on the tray, then beamed at Rolf as he took it from her and carried it to the kitchen.

Kay picked up her brushes, and although she expected him to return to the upper ceiling he did not do so immediately. Instead he came back and stood watching her make careful brush strokes. She was deeply conscious of his presence beside her, although his observation did not trouble her because she was becoming accustomed to him standing near by while she worked.

There was silence in the room until Estelle spoke to him. 'Rolf, do you know that Kay hasn't mentioned a word to Ivy about—*you know what*?'

'I know what?' he queried lazily. 'What am I supposed to know?'

'I'm talking about your flat,' she explained impatiently.

'Stell, there are times when you talk too much,' he drawled, then turned to Kay with a change of subject. 'I'll be interested to see the progress at the end of today's sitting. In the meantime I'll return to my friends up top—the spiders.'

Estelle broke her pose to turn to him anxiously. 'I hope you haven't found any wood borer up there. I mean, *we* don't want borer.'

'Nobody wants borer,' he returned easily. 'Fortunately, good heart timber has prevented them from burrowing in and holding hands to keep the house standing.' He left them and made his way up the stairs.

Estelle said, 'He must have his little joke, but it would

be serious if *our house* were to be infested by borer.'

Kay merely smiled, refusing to allow herself to become goaded into making a reply, and after that very little was said between them. She was thankful when the sitting ended, although she could see that the work was coming along nicely, and she felt that one more Saturday would enable her to complete it to her satisfaction.

When Estelle left the model's chair she stretched, then came to look at herself on the easel. 'Gosh, you sure know what you're doing,' she admitted with reluctant admiration.

'You're an excellent model,' Kay told her generously. 'Your eyes have hardly wandered from the spot I gave you as a focus point.'

'That's because I was really looking at Rolf, although he wasn't there today,' she said with a hint of disappointment. 'By the way, that dishwasher he mentioned—I suppose it's too much to hope it's been put in?'

Kay's brows rose. 'Are you saying our dishwasher is of vital importance to you?'

'Of course it is, and please stop pretending you don't know why.'

Kay shrugged. 'Then you'll be glad to know it was installed this week.' She knew exactly why the dishwasher was of such interest to Estelle, but had no wish to hear the words uttered.

'Oh, really? I must see it,' exclaimed Estelle eagerly, and without further invitation she hurried through to the kitchen.

Moments later Kay heard a squeal of delight and could imagine Estelle peering inside the new appliance while talking to Ivy. When she returned her mood appeared to be highly cheerful, even to the extent of favouring Kay with a smile as she confided, 'Ivy says that you and Rolf have been going swimming each day.'

'Yes, that's right.' Kay dipped a brush in turpentine, then wiped it on a paint rag.

A green glitter appeared in Estelle's eyes but she continued to sound cheerful as she declared with a determined air, 'Today I shall come with you. I suppose you go at high tide?'

'Yes, we do.' Kay felt a surge of despondency, knowing that today's swim with Rolf would be entirely ruined.

Estelle went on, 'High tide is at four o'clock today, so you can tell Rolf I'll be here at that time and then we can go down to the sea together.' The words were uttered in the form of a command. 'You will tell him?' The green eyes held a glitter of doubt as they rested upon Kay.

'I'll tell him,' Kay promised, hoping her voice didn't betray the depression building within her. 'Actually, I can't understand why you don't tell him yourself.'

'Because I want him to know we're *friends*.' A beaming smile swept over her face while she clasped Kay's hand in an unexpected gesture. 'It's so much nicer to be able to swim with friends,' she gushed.

'Yes, I suppose so.' Kay was unimpressed by Estelle's sudden warmth towards her. Somehow it lacked sincerity.

'Then you'll be sure to tell him? Promise you'll tell him you think we should swim together.' The smile came again.

'I've said I'll tell him.' Kay felt irritable as she watched Estelle leave the house, and she wondered why Ivy had found it necessary to mention the swimming sessions. In a vague way they had developed into an almost sacred ritual which was now about to become desecrated.

But there was no need to question Ivy, who had little difficulty in sensing Kay's disappointment. 'I'm afraid it was her mother, dear,' she explained. 'Mrs Lexington-Barron was passing this way to the corner shop when she saw you both frolicking in the water. So when Estelle asked me if you and Rolf went swimming each day it was useless for me to deny it.'

'Of course. Quite useless.'

'And she knew it wouldn't be after high tide because of the undertow out there. At times the drag can pull a swimmer beneath the waves.' Ivy added warningly as she returned to the kitchen to prepare lunch.

When Rolf came downstairs Kay noticed he had changed into a fresh cream shirt. The short sleeves revealed his forearms, and as she took one swift peep at the rippling muscles she recalled their strength while holding her close to his body.

The memory caused a queer little sensation in the pit of her stomach, and she knew it was unwise to dwell upon such moments, therefore she forced a casual note into her voice as she watched his perusal of the portrait. 'The model sends you a message.'

'The model is almost beginning to speak from the canvas. What sort of message would this be?'

'She says she'll swim with us at four o'clock.'

'She won't, you know.'

'Do you mean you think she'll change her mind? She was surprisingly friendly towards me just before she left. She even smiled at me. It was the sort of smile she—she reserves for you.'

'Really?' He left the portrait and went into the studio where he stood frowning at the house plan on his drawing-board.

Kay followed him, drawn to his side as though by an unseen magnet. 'I couldn't help wondering if perhaps——' She fell silent.

He turned to regard her, his blue eyes kindling with interest. 'Yes? If perhaps——?'

Kay hesitated then said, 'If perhaps she's feeling less antagonistic towards me.'

His dark brows rose. 'Why should she be antagonistic

towards you?'

'You're saying you don't know?'

He frowned. 'I'm saying she has no reason to be antagonistic towards you.'

She bit her lip as she thought about his words. No reason to feel antagonistic. To be more specific, that meant that Estelle had no reason to feel *jealous* of her because she held no high place in Rolf's thoughts.

The knowledge was depressing, but she managed to keep her voice even as she reminded him of the situation. 'You're forgetting that she wants to see Ivy and me leave this house. That's why her sudden show of friendship came as a surprise.'

He shrugged and turned back to his house plan, then lifted a ruler to check line measurements.

But she persisted. 'Just tell me why you're so sure she won't be swimming with us at four o'clock, and then I'll leave you to get on with your work.'

He laid down the ruler then said patiently, 'It's because we'll not be swimming at that hour. The tide will be on its way out.'

'She said high tide is at four.'

'She's mistaken. Today's high tide is at two-thirty. I heard the tidal report come over the air.'

'Oh, then I'd better let her know.' She left him and went to the phone, but although she listened for several minutes to the rhythmic sound at the other end there was no reply, and eventually she replaced the receiver.

A short time before two-thirty she made another attempt to phone Estelle, but still there was no reply, and, sighing, she knew that the redhead would be furious to learn they had swum without her. The new friendship, if indeed it existed, would be at an end.

By that time Kay was wearing her yellow swimsuit, its high-hipped backless brevity covered by a short towelling wrap as they walked across the road to the stony shore where she dropped it near the water's edge.

Rolf also divested himself of a cotton pullover that reached the top of his legs, but before letting it fall to the shingle he stood immobile with it slung carelessly behind his shoulder while gazing out to sea.

The frown on his face told Kay he was deep in thought, and watching him she was reminded of Michelangelo's statue of David. It was an effort to drag her eyes away from the tanned broad shoulders, flat stomach and narrow hips, but she forced herself to make her way into the water, which was calm, almost tepid, and soothing to her disturbed mind.

He joined her within moments, and for the next half-hour they splashed, laughed and swam. When near enough to touch him she longed to place her hand on his shining wet skin, but she resisted the temptation. She ached with an intense yearning to feel his tanned fingers find their way to her breast, but they did not come within yards of her body until a rising wave threw her against him.

That seemed to herald the end of the idyllic moments, because Rolf moved away abruptly as he said, 'That's enough—I must get back to work.'

'Work?' Disappointment made her feel dazed.

'I have plans of movable houses to complete, remember? I spent all this morning up in the loft, and now I must make up for lost time.' He turned and made his way to the shore.

She followed reluctantly, feeling as though the sun had lost its warmth, and wondering if he had tired of her company. This thought became even more definite when they reached home and he hurried upstairs to dress. A short time later he was in the studio, his concentration indicating he had no wish to be disturbed.

Kay took the hint. She worked quietly, adding extra touches to the portrait's background and deepening the shadows in the folds of the dress. She emphasised lights in the hair, and by four o'clock she had become so engrossed she failed to notice Estelle's arrival until Ivy ushered her into the lounge.

The multicoloured wrap worn by Estelle fell from her shoulders to her hips in the form of a gay cape, and it seemed obvious she wore her swimsuit beneath it. Her long shapely legs were bare, and on her feet she wore sandals for walking over the stones.

Ivy sent a troubled look towards Kay. 'I've told her you've already been for your swim.'

Kay sent Estelle an apologetic smile. 'I'm sorry, but I'm afraid you made a mistake with the tidal time. I tried to phone you . . .'

'Mother and I went out to lunch,' Estelle explained, then asked, 'Where's Rolf? Don't tell me he's still up in the loft.'

Rolf came to the studio doorway. 'No, he is not still up in the loft,' he said drily.

Estelle gave a cry of pleasure. 'Ah, there you are! Rolf dear, let's go swimming.'

He spoke patiently, 'I've already been for a swim, and now I have work to do.'

Estelle pouted. 'But I've come *expecting* to go swimming. Just take a good look at me—I'm ready for the water.' She unfastened the cape and allowed it to fall to the floor where it lay in a colourful heap. Apart from the brevity of a small bikini, its loss left her almost naked.

A shocked gasp escaped Ivy but she said nothing, while Kay's artistic urge sent her thoughts towards figure sketching. However, she was also aware that Rolf's eyes were resting upon the rounded mounds of full breasts and the barely concealed nudity of the lovely redhead. She knew that a fleeting smile played about his lips, and she wondered if the sight of Estelle's body filled him with delight.

Estelle's lithe steps took her across the room to stand closer to Rolf. 'Take me swimming,' she requested again, smiling up into his face.

His features became inscrutable as he regarded the perfection of her figure. 'You're really quite beautiful, Stell.'

Her smile broadened with satisfaction. 'I'm glad you think so.' Then, despite the presence of the others, she added quietly, 'I really wanted to show you that I'm now—grown up. So shall we go?'

His expression did not change. 'I'm afraid I have work to do. Nor is the tide to my liking.'

'It won't be the first time we've swum with an outgoing tide.'

'That happens to be how I know of its dangers,' he pointed out.

'We can cope with it,' she argued.

'Maybe, but I'm not sure that Kay can.'

'Oh, well, is it so very necessary for her to come with us?'

Kay sent her a bleak stare. So much for closer relations with Estelle, she thought, then held her breath as she awaited Rolf's reply.

When it came it was non-committal. 'You're becoming deaf, Stell, old dear,' he drawled teasingly. 'I *said* I have *work* to do.'

Estelle's deep sigh betrayed frustration. 'To the devil with your work. People take a break at weekends.'

'You're forgetting I have a job to do within a limited time—and without interruptions,' he snapped.

Estelle became scathing. 'Are you trying to tell me that Kay doesn't interrupt your concentration? I'll bet she's in and out of the studio on any pretence.'

'Kay respects my need for complete absorption,' he told Estelle mildly. 'She doesn't disturb me in the least.'

His last words hit Kay with a force that hurt. He could put a ring round *that* statement, she thought with an overflow of bitterness. He doesn't even know I'm here.

Estelle spoke with ill-concealed exasperation. 'You could have concentrated at our place.'

Rolf sighed. 'You're forgetting that Ivy's kind invitation has enabled me to examine the state of this house.' Then his voice hardened. 'You're beginning to make me feel weary, Stell.'

'In that case I might as well go home,' she snapped coldly.

'An excellent idea,' he grinned.

Listening to their conversation, Kay guessed that Estelle's temper was being bitten back only with difficulty. And she also realised that here was a case where two people had known each other too well for too long.

Years ago, when Rolf had stayed at Hope House during school holidays, they had become like brother and sister, but while Rolf had continued to regard Estelle with the camaraderie of those days, Estelle had advanced beyond it. She now longed for a closer relationship, one that meant a ring on her finger—if only she could get him to the stage of placing it there.

Would the day dawn when Rolf woke up to the fact that he loved Estelle? The thought caused a sharp ache somewhere deep down within her, and then she became aware that Estelle was speaking to her.

'Kay, dear, next Saturday we'll go swimming for sure. Promise?'

Kay gave a faint smile, knowing that this show of friendship was for Rolf's benefit. 'Yes, I suppose so,' was all she said.

'I want us to be *friends*,' Estelle gushed as though making an effort to drive home the point, then, turning back to the tall man, she exclaimed, 'Rolf, I almost forgot—Mother *insists* that you come to dinner with us this evening. She has something to discuss with you.'

He frowned. 'Oh? What is it?'

Estelle became mysterious. 'She needs your advice

and your help.'

The dark brows shot up as he echoed mockingly, 'Mrs Lexington-Barron needs my advice and help? As I recall, it was always she who told me what to do—and if I'm not mistaken she's still making the effort to guide my movements.'

Estelle ignored his last words as she smiled archly. 'It's about a party. She needs someone to act as host.'

Kay became conscious of another dull ache. Was this to be an engagement party? Had Estelle's plans for her future with Rolf advanced further than she realised?

Rolf said, 'Very well, if Ivy will excuse me this evening I'll see what I can do for your mother.' He picked up Estelle's cape from where it had remained on the floor, then said bluntly, 'Put this on or you'll go down with an ague or some such plague.'

'Rubbish,' Estelle snapped crossly, but obeyed by flinging it about her shoulders. 'I thought you'd *like* to see me in my bikini,' she added with a degree of petulance.

'I think we've all had our fill,' he told her drily.

Estelle ignored the taunt concerning her nudity. 'OK, we'll see you at six o'clock.' The cape swirled in a colourful circle as she swung round and left the lounge with barely a nod towards Kay or Ivy.

Her departure left a strained silence, broken by the unnecessary bang of the front door. Rolf then returned to the studio, while Ivy almost stamped out to the kitchen.

Kay followed her to whisper urgently, 'Don't let her upset you.'

But Ivy made no effort to hide her seething anger. '*Upset* me? She makes me mad! Brazen, that's what I call it,' she hissed furiously. 'Throwing her naked body at him in that blatant manner.'

'But it wasn't naked. She wore a bikini,' Kay defended her.

'Huh! What did those three small triangles hide?'

'Nothing much—but it's a beautiful body. I'd like to paint it.'

'Is that so? Then let me tell you that yours is just as good. In fact, it's better, I'd say.'

Kay laughed. 'You haven't seen my body.'

'That's what you think. That glass door to the upstairs shower hides nothing. Didn't I walk in on you one day not so long ago?'

'Yes, well, I hadn't locked the bathroom door because neither of us ever bothers to do so.'

'Which means we must remember to do so in future. We have the man of the house with us at present.'

Kay sent her a glance that was full of curiosity. 'You're already looking upon him as the man of the house?'

Ivy ignored the question, brushing it aside as she put forth another query. 'Tell me, what's this party in aid of? That's what I'd like to know.'

Kay shrugged, but did not admit that she also would like to know. However, unless Rolf confided in her she was likely to remain in ignorance. Or perhaps he'd tell Ivy, who was taking an interest in the set of house plans he was compiling. Lately their heads had been together while discussing cupboards and space for vacuum cleaners and brooms.

Nor was there any doubt of the fact that they both missed his presence at the table during the evening meal, the sight of the empty chair giving Kay an instinctive understanding of Ivy's despair when Arnold no longer sat in it.

Later when she went to bed she lay staring at the brilliance of the heavens while thoughts of Rolf and Estelle continued to hover in her mind. 'What are they doing at this moment?' she asked a bright cluster, unaware that she had spoken aloud.

Estelle means a star, its twinkle seemed to remind her.

How could she fail to light her way into his heart?

Stop it, you fool, she told herself crossly, then sat up abruptly to switch on the light and snatch at a book. But concentration was short-lived and eventually a glance at her watch showed the hands creeping towards midnight. Restlessly, she decided that perhaps a hot drink would help to combat this sleeplessness, therefore she slipped out of bed and flung on a white nylon wrap which hung loosely over her flimsy, almost transparent white nightgown.

In the passage she paused briefly to listen at Ivy's door, but the faint snore that came to her ears indicated that the older woman slept soundly and was in no need of a soothing Horlicks.

Kay then hurried towards the stairs, and as she descended, the wrap fluttered behind her like a small white cloud; nor was there any need to fasten it, because she intended to be in the kitchen for only a few minutes before carrying the hot drink upstairs to her bedroom.

But even as she stood beside the stove waiting for the milk to heat she was startled by the sound of footsteps, and the next instant Rolf walked into the kitchen, entering through the back door. His unexpected appearance caused her to drag the flimsy wrap across the front of the revealing nightgown, and, searching for words, she said weakly, 'Oh, so you're home. I didn't expect——'

'Yes, I've come home.' His eyes kindled as they took in the scantiness of her attire.

Had there been something significant about the way he had uttered the word *home*? she wondered. Or had this been her imagination? Aloud she said, 'You've had a pleasant evening?'

'It was—interesting,' he admitted in a casual tone that told her nothing.

'Interesting? That's a word one hears in an art gallery.'

He frowned. 'What do you mean?'

'People who don't know what to say when asked for their opinion of a painting usually declare it to be *interesting*. It's a word that conceals what they really think about it.'

'Which means you're accusing me of concealing my feeling about this evening,' he parried.

'Well, aren't you?'

'Not really.' He was silent for several moments then admitted, 'It's just that I'm vaguely puzzled.'

'In what way? Estelle said her mother needed help with drink and catering arrangements, didn't she?'

'That part was easy enough, but there was something else. I sensed she had a further plan in mind, something about which she was very cagey, although she gave me the impression I was supposed to know all about it.'

'Is there a special reason for this party?' Kay asked casually.

'I presume she's merely returning hospitality.'

Kay took a deep breath, then asked, 'Are you sure it's not an—engagement party that is being planned?'

His brow became thunderous as he rasped, 'I doubt that even Mrs Lexington-Barron would imagine she could twist my arm to that extent.'

'Then you'll just have to wait and see what sort of a surprise she comes up with,' Kay told him sweetly. 'I recall Estelle saying that her mother usually gets her own way.'

Instead of replying he took milk from the fridge, then changed the subject by saying, 'I'll join you with a hot drink, and by the way, is Ivy satisfied with this electric stove?'

The question surprised her. 'Yes, I think so. It seems to do all she requires of it. Why do you ask?' she queried casually.

'Estelle feels she should have a new one, something more modern with a flat ceramic top.'

A laugh escaped Kay. 'How sweet of Estelle to be so thoughtful for Ivy.'

'Perhaps Estelle is more thoughtful than you imagine.'

Kay controlled her impatience with difficulty. 'Did she have any other kitchen improvements in mind?'

'Well, she thinks a larger deep freeze would be an asset.' He turned to examine the small chest-type of freezer with its lift-up lid. 'Don't you think a larger upright type with a door would be better? I mean the cupboard style.'

'This also being Estelle's suggestion?' The question came quietly.

'As it happens, she did mention it.'

The milk he had added to hers took little time to heat, and Kay now snatched the pot from the element before it could boil over. She filled the mugs and placed them on a small tray, the action giving her time to think about Estelle's subtle plans for improved appliances in the kitchen.

He took the tray from her and carried it into the lounge where he placed it on the small table beside the settee, but before sitting down he took her painting-smock from the studio. Handing it to her, he said, 'I know the night is warm, but you'd be wise to put this on as an extra covering.' The words held a hint of command.

'You're afraid I'll go down with an ague or some such plague?' she smiled, repeating his earlier words to Estelle, yet needled by the knowledge that the sight of her in flimsy nylon had little or no effect upon him.

'I've no wish to see you catch a chill,' he told her bluntly.

'At least not before the portrait's finished,' she shot back at him.

He sent her a quizzical look. 'Do I detect irritation for some reason?'

She forced a smile. 'Of course not. What could possibly irritate me?' Then, sitting on the settee beside him, she added, 'This is not what I expected. I intended taking my hot drink up to bed.'

'The unexpected is apt to pop up and alter the trend of events,' he reminded her. 'But you haven't told me if you think Ivy would like to have a new stove and a larger deep freeze.'

'Such expense would send her reeling backwards.'

'That's why I'm anxious to discuss it with you before her objections are poured on the idea.'

Kay's brown eyes questioned him across the rim of her mug. 'Tell me honestly, is it really Ivy's wishes that are being questioned? Isn't it a matter of what Estelle desires to see installed in the kitchen?'

'For Pete's sake, what makes you so sure about that?'

She became exasperated. 'Because I suspect you're about to become engaged to her. Why can't you be honest enough to admit that the party discussed this evening is really an engagement party? And these suggestions of a new stove and larger deep freeze—do you really expect me to believe they're for *Ivy*? You must think I'm daft.'

'Why do you say that?' His tone had become icy.

'Because it's obvious Estelle wants them for herself, all nicely installed before she moves into this house.'

He became alert. 'Oh? When is that to be?'

'When you're married to her, of course.' She almost choked on the words as the mere thought filled her with fury.

'Now I know you *are* daft,' he snapped crisply.

She shook her head in silence, feeling utterly miserable.

He went on, 'I can only repeat that the party discussed this evening had nothing to do with an engagement. It's merely an occasion when Mrs Lexington-Barron intends to entertain a number of guests. Further, it's her birthday. Surely it's possible for her to arrange a birthday party for herself without other people jumping to conclusions concerning her motive?' he gritted impatiently.

'People in high places?' she giggled, making an effort to hide the sweeping wave of relief. 'No doubt you were able to advise her on the liquid refreshments to be ordered, but Estelle also said she needed help. What form will this take?'

'She has asked me to act as her host,' he admitted abruptly.

'Ah, the future son-in-law. Very fitting.' The words had just slipped out.

He turned to her, making no attempt to hide his anger. 'It's beyond me to understand why you persist with this engagement idea.'

'Then you'll forgive me if the time comes when I say *I told you so*. Incidentally, when is this party to take place?'

'On Saturday week,' he almost snarled, then startled her with an abrupt question. 'Tell me, why does my engagement to Estelle concern you so deeply?'

'It doesn't,' she snapped.

'You're lying,' he accused her. 'Please don't try to deny it because the fact comes through in a way that can only be termed loud and clear.'

She licked dry lips while trying to find an answer. 'It's for Ivy's sake,' she hedged at last. 'From the moment it's made public she'll feel she must vacate this house, and for her it will be like leaving her beloved Arnold.'

'It's probably the wisest course for her to take,' he declared flatly. 'She can't live with a ghost for ever. The time will come when she must pull herself together and get back to reality.'

'I suppose you're right,' sighed Kay. 'But I can't help feeling sad for her.' An involuntary shiver passed through her as she visualised Ivy's pending unhappiness.

It did not escape Rolf's notice. 'You're cold,' he said, taking the empty mug from her hand and placing it with his own on the table.

'The air has become cooler, and I haven't much on.'

'I must say it suits you very nicely.'

'It's time I went back to bed.'

'First allow me to offer a little of my own bodily warmth. I've plenty to spare,' he grinned, shrugging off his jacket, and moving closer he placed it about her shoulders.

His nearness made her feel tense, causing her to hold her breath as she waited for him to draw back. But he did not do so. Instead he remained close, staring down into her face while silence lasted between them; a silence seething with tension.

It seemed to last an age, and she found herself unable to drag her gaze from the shadowed blue eyes with their subdued glitter. And when she felt his arms drawing her against him she was unaware of the contented sigh that escaped to betray her and whisper of her sudden excitement that was spiked by an inner joy.

It caused him to lower his head, seeking lips that parted to his seductive teasing while his fingers smoothed the auburn strands of hair from her face. They fondled her ear, then traced a line down her jaw, and as they stroked her throat she became engulfed in a warmth that made her pulses throb.

In a daze she felt his mouth leave her lips to trail across her brow and cheeks, then return to part them once more, and as the kiss deepened she knew his hands had found their way beneath the jacket and painting-smock, moving over her body with a gentle kneading that sent a flame of desire flaring through her bloodstream.

She became conscious of his ragged breathing and knew that his heart thumped with sledgehammer precision, and above the inferno raging within her body she was vaguely aware that he had deftly changed their positions on the settee so that they were now almost lying along its length.

His voice in her ear muttered huskily, 'Darling, you know how I feel about you.'

Ecstasy filled her. He had called her *darling*. But she shook her head. 'No, how can I know? I had the impression you looked upon me as being one filled with cunning.'

'Those doubts have long since gone. Nor were they more than superficial.'

'You could have fooled me.'

His mouth on hers silenced her, and then he murmured, 'Doesn't this tell you I want you, that I'm longing to carry you up into the realms of bliss?'

She nodded dumbly, unable to speak while his hands on her buttocks crushed her body against his, making her fully aware of his arousal. And as her arms wound about him his lips trailed about her throat, then found their way to her breast. Pushing aside the flimsy nylon, they nibbled at her raised nipple until small moans of delight escaped her.

'Now, darling, now,' he groaned, almost in desperation.

Darling. He had said it again. And she longed, oh, how she longed to let the liquid fire in her veins take control, to abandon herself to the passion waiting to be unleashed by their lovemaking. But even as her yearning for their bodies to merge became more intense the silence of the room was shattered by a faint though unmistakable sound from above.

It brought Kay to her senses. 'Ivy's awake and out of bed,' she gasped. 'She might come downstairs.'

'Don't panic, I'd say that's most unlikely,' he soothed.

'It is not. She'll notice I've left my light on, so she's

sure to look in to see if I'm reading or if I've fallen asleep with it still burning.'

She struggled away from the clasp of his arms, then rolled to the floor with a slight thud. Her wrap fluttered behind her while she ran across the room, but she dragged it about her as she sped up the stairs, reaching the landing as Ivy emerged from her room.

'Ah, there you are, dear, the older woman said. 'I wondered where you were. I was about to come down to look for you.'

'I couldn't sleep, so I made Horlicks.'

'Is Rolf home yet?'

'Yes, he came in a short time ago.'

Ivy looked at her critically. 'You're sounding very breathless, dear, and you look quite flushed. I'd say it's no wonder if he caught you in that skimpy attire. It's almost transparent.'

'Yes, I'm afraid it is. Would you like me to make you a hot drink?'

'No, thank you, not if it means your going downstairs like that.'

'Very well, I'll go to bed.' Kay kissed her lightly and moments later had flung herself between the sheets where she again lay gazing at the stars, her mind in a turmoil as she recalled the pressure of his lips on hers, the feel of his arms clasping her against him.

Had she fallen in love with him? Or had her longing for him merely sent her into a state of rapturous bliss that could be mistaken for love? *Darling*, he had whispered. But that didn't mean he had any depth of feeling for her. It was just part of a softening process towards his goal of satisfying his needs. And she had been ready to submit, would have submitted but for the noise upstairs. How could something so momentous be prevented by something so mundane?

CHAPTER EIGHT

WHEN Kay woke next morning the stars had been replaced by clouds scudding across the blue, and as she recalled the events of the previous evening she became engulfed by an acute shyness. She dreaded the thought of going downstairs to face Rolf, and although she racked her brain for a plausible excuse to remain in her room, she could think of no convincing reason for doing so.

She took extra time over her shower and dressing, and when she felt sure that Rolf would have had his breakfast and become busy in the studio, she made her way downstairs to the kitchen.

Ivy was there, pouring herself a second cup of tea. She had finished her breakfast and she now greeted Kay with a warm smile. 'Ah, there you are, dear. You're late this morning. Did you sleep longer than usual?'

'A little, perhaps.' She put two slices of bread in the pop-up toaster, then asked casually, 'Rolf has had his breakfast?'

'Not yet. He's out jogging. Estelle called for him quite early.'

'Estelle?' Kay swung round to stare at Ivy.

'Yes. She was wearing one of those track-suits with white stripes down the arms and legs. Turquoise. It looked really smart against her flaming red hair.'

'Did it, indeed?' Kay felt a surge of anger. 'And so he went with her like a shot from a gun.' Bitterness tinged the words.

'I think he felt he needed the exercise.' Ivy sounded complacent.

'Exercise? Huh!' Kay thought of the previous

evening. Had he known he would be jogging with Estelle first thing in the morning?

Ivy flashed a look of interest towards her. 'You've become quite flushed, dear. You wouldn't be just a teeny weeny bit jealous, would you?' The question came softly.

Kay tossed her head haughtily. 'Not at all,' she lied. *Jealous*? Of course she was jealous. It burned within her like bitter gall, but she also knew it was something she must control.

Ivy went on, 'You must remember he was their guest last night, so when she called to ask him to go jogging it wouldn't have been polite to have refused such a simple request.'

'Are you saying it hadn't been previously arranged?'

'I don't think so. He seemed surprised to see her.'

'How long have they been away?' Kay found difficulty in keeping the agitation from her voice.

'Oh, at least an hour. They should be back quite soon.'

This prophecy proved to be correct when Rolf and Estelle came in the back door a short time later, the latter's face aglow with what could only be termed satisfaction.

Rolf said, 'We have a guest for breakfast, if that's OK with you, Ivy.'

Estelle took a quick glance at the dishes on the bench then sent a winning smile towards Ivy as she chimed in, 'I can see that you and Kay have had your breakfast, so there's no need for you to bother about us. I'll fix something for Rolf and me, so why don't you both just leave us to it?' And with those words she filled the electric kettle to make fresh tea.

Ivy went slightly pale as she looked from Rolf to Estelle, but she said nothing. Nor did it appear as if she could do other than stand by helplessly until suddenly it seemed as if the sight of her kitchen being taken over was just too much. Her face lost more of its colour, and with her mouth gripped in a thin line she hurried towards the stairs.

Kay was aware of Ivy's distress but knew there was little she could say or do to comfort the older woman. She watched Estelle take what she needed from cupboards and the fridge, and within a short time the odour of bacon, eggs and tomatoes sizzling in the pan infuriated her to the extent of making her long to push the redhead aside while she herself prepared their breakfast.

But to do so would be more than enough to betray the anger and jealousy seething within her, and to make matters worse she knew that Rolf was regarding her with quizzical interest, almost as though deliberately watching her reaction to the scene.

The look in his eyes caused her to take a grip on herself, and leaving the room abruptly she went to the studio which was always the best place for control of mind. It was the place where most irritations vanished the moment she picked up a brush.

Leafing through a few sketches, she selected one that was awaiting to have its colour applied, then squeezed out blobs of raw umber, cobalt and vermilion watercolour. Washes for a grey sky with touches of blue were floated on to the dampened paper, and they were almost dry when Rolf walked into the room.

He examined the painted sky critically, then regarded her serious face. 'Those dark masses reflect the clouds in your own thoughts?' he asked lazily.

She forced herself to smile. 'Who says I have dark clouds in my mind?'

'I do. They're hovering all about you. They're coming out of your ears like black smoke from a diesel engine.'

She refused to find amusement in the remark, nor was it easy to conceal the extent of her indignation. 'Let's just say I feel sad for Ivy. That blatant takeover of her kitchen has upset her.'

'Not to any great extent, I hope.'

'Can't you see that it represented the thin edge of the wedge? It was a tangible display of events to come. However, it might jolt her into facing up to reality.'

'And what about you? Are you also ready to face the inevitable?'

'I'm young enough to face anything. If you're about to take steps to toss us out of this house——'

'Take steps?' he prompted smoothly.

'Enlist the aid of the law for possession, of course.'

'You're so sure I'll do that?' His voice had become crisp.

'Well, if you do I can take it in my stride. But Ivy's different. She's upstairs, probably weeping while she asks Arnold's advice.'

'Let's hope the old boy knows which way the wind is blowing so that he can advise her wisely.'

Kay sent him a bleak look. 'At the moment that same wind is making a mighty cold draught round these parts,' she retorted pointedly.

'I didn't notice any draughts of a chilly nature last night.' The words came in a smooth murmur.

She was unable to look at him while she said crossly, 'I must have been out of my mind. I should have realised you'd just returned from visiting Estelle where—where you'd probably become frustrated by her mother's continued presence.'

Blue sparks glittered through his narrowed lids, but the retort that rose to his lips was silenced as Estelle's voice reached them.

'Rolf, *dear*, breakfast is ready, come and get it or I'll throw it out.'

Kay's smile became filled with sweetness. 'You'd better run along, *Rolf dear*.'

He scowled at her. 'I'll deal with you later.'

She was startled. 'Deal with me? What do you mean?'

'You'll find out eventually, Kay Carlson. Just you wait and see,' he gritted, then he strode from the room.

During the next week his words remained in her mind, but although she waited to be dealt with the days were uneventful and it appeared as if he had forgotten the threat.

She decided that this was because he was throwing himself into his work by spending his days and evenings in the studio, a deep frown marring his brow as he leaned over his drawing-board. And despite the fact that she worked near by it seemed as though they were in separate rooms.

There were times when Kay left her own work, moving to stand beside him for a closer examination of the plans for these special houses that would be constructed in a builder's yard and later carried by heavy transport to their permanent site. But her interest drew little response from him, and there were even times when she imagined he deliberately stepped away from her.

On Monday and Tuesday she took little notice of his attitude, deciding that he had spent so many hours examining Hope House, from every inch of the wiring to the plumbing, and that he was now making up for lost time.

However, by Wednesday she felt vaguely hurt, and was even longing to be *dealt* with—anything but this, this state of being constantly shut away from him. But it was not until Thursday that she realised she was being dealt with by being ignored as far as politeness would permit.

By Friday her frustration was at its highest. Concentration on her work was impossible and she made silly mistakes with the watercolour in hand, even to the extent of knocking over the jar of water in which she washed her brushes. To make matters worse, her depression conveyed itself to Rolf.

'Something is troubling you?' he asked blandly.

'What makes you think so?'

'Constant sighs usually indicate low spirits.'

She shrugged, then nodded towards the portrait of Estelle. 'I'll be glad when tomorrow comes. I'm keen to finish it, and to get it out of my sight,' she added with more bitterness than she realised.

'Why? Aren't you pleased with it?'

'You're the one it must satisfy,' she responded coolly.

'How long will it take to dry?'

'Several days. Yellow often takes ages, but it can take its own sweet time, hanging on your wall. I presume it'll have a place of honour in your flat?'

'Actually I intend it to be gift-wrapped.'

'And no doubt presented to Estelle with a dozen red roses?' It was difficult to conceal the hurt growing steadily within her.

'Now that's a darned good idea.'

'Or she might prefer an attractive dried arrangement,' Kay suggested through tight lips. 'Roses have a limited life, whereas dried flowers would last for ages to remind her of this—this momentous occasion,' she added, twisting the knife within herself.

'Yes, that's an even better idea,' he approved. 'I'll order some from the florist and they can be presented to her sitting on the flat parcel.'

'A most impressive gift, but why bother to wrap it when she has already seen it?'

'Oh, well, this is to be a special occasion,' he grinned.

'I'll bet it will,' she snapped coldly.

He regarded her intently. 'Something is obviously annoying you. Would you begrudge me the pleasure of presenting the gift in a manner that will give the recipient the greatest delight?'

'No, of course not.' Lucky Estelle, she thought, fighting to control a surge of overwhelming jealousy

that made her want to scream. And then another
thought caused her to say, 'I really believed this portrait
to be for you, to be hung on your own wall, but if it's
for Estelle I dare say it means the same thing.'

'I'm sure she'll enjoy looking at it,' he returned
quietly. 'You've made her face as beautiful as it really
is.'

'Thank you.' She almost choked on the words.

'Be careful tomorrow. I mean, don't ruin it by adding
too many final touches.'

'I'll watch my brush strokes,' she promised, then left
the room before he could see the sudden gathering of
moisture in her eyes.

Saturday dawned with a clear sky which gave promise of
another warm summer day, and when Kay went into the
studio before mid-morning she was surprised to find
Estelle already there.

'I just walked in,' the redhead admitted casually. 'I
know it's not yet ten o'clock, but I want to talk to Rolf.
Where is he?'

Kay gave a faint shrug. 'I'm afraid I've no idea.' Did
Estelle imagine she already owned Hope House and that
she had the right to walk in and out as she pleased? she
wondered uneasily.

'I came early specially to talk to him,' Estelle declared
crossly. 'Mother is becoming impatient with us both.'

'Oh?' Kay held her breath, waiting for further
information.

'There's only a week left before the party, and
nothing is settled.'

'Settled? You mean about the catering and ordering
of drinks?'

'No, of course not.' Estelle became impatient. 'I
mean about *us*, nothing is settled between Rolf and me.'

'Are you referring to your engagement?'

'Naturally. What else?' The words were snapped.

Kay decided she must be imagining this conversation, and to get things clearly sorted in her own mind she persisted, 'Are you saying you've come early to get your engagement to Rolf definitely settled?'

'That's right. You're beginning to see the light.'

'But aren't you mistaking the year? This is not leap year, when girls are supposed to have the prerogative to propose to a man.'

'Don't be stupid,' Estelle hissed. 'I'm not actually proposing—the situation is different between Rolf and me.'

'Oh? In what way?' Kay's tone had become bleak.

'Well, when Daddy was alive Rolf promised him he'd always take care of me.'

'Wasn't that when you were children, and you were inclined to do rash things? I'm sure it didn't mean he was to be responsible for you for life.'

An enigmatic smile crossed Estelle's face. 'Mother has reminded Rolf of his promise. It was just before Daddy died, therefore it was like a sacred deathbed promise.'

Kay was appalled. 'I've never heard such rubbish.'

'Then you'll just have to wait and see, won't you?'

'You can't possibly mean she intends to bully him into making an announcement at the party?'

'Why not? It would make it a wonderful occasion, especially as it's her birthday. It would be like giving her something she wants more than anything else.'

'We can't have everything we want in this life,' Kay pointed out, hating the thought of Rolf and Estelle becoming engaged, then she took heart as his virile form flashed before her eyes. 'In any case, I don't believe for one moment that Rolf is a man who can be bullied into anything.'

Estelle's chin rose haughtily. 'You've no right to use the word bullied, and believe me, Mother usually gets her own way.'

'And no doubt so do you. Estelle, I'm beginning to suspect you don't know Rolf very well.'

The words caused laughter. 'Don't be daft, I've known him for years and years.'

'You've been *acquainted* with him for years,' Kay corrected, 'but if you imagine you can force him into announcing his engagement before he's ready to do so, then believe me, you don't know him at all.'

Estelle remained confident. 'It's Mother's wish for it to happen at her party, and if I know Mother that's when it will happen.'

The subject was beginning to make Kay feel positively ill, and she feared that if it continued her work would be affected, therefore she said, 'Suppose we make a start?'

'Yes, let's get on with it. I'm tired of these sittings and am glad this is the last.'

'That makes two of us,' Kay said wearily.

'Of course I'm delighted that Rolf wants to have a portrait of me. Don't you think it proves he's in love with me?'

'Yes, I think it does,' Kay agreed, trying to keep sadness from her voice yet knowing she must face up to the inevitable. Nor was she anxious to delve into the reason for this state of mind, therefore she worked in silence, her steady concentration sweeping all other problems from her thoughts.

Estelle also remained silent until Rolf came in during the coffee-break, and then she brightened visibly. She drew him aside to whisper urgently, and as Kay watched them she noticed his face become an inscrutable mask.

Had he sensed he was about to be cajoled into making the announcement of their engagement? she wondered. But despite her scrutiny she was unable to assess his reaction to whatever Estelle had suggested because his attitude betrayed nothing more than polite interest.

It was almost noon before she finally laid down her brushes. 'I can't see that I can do any more to it,' she said, a deep sigh of weariness escaping her as she moved the easel to a position beside Estelle's chair.

Rolf left his drawing-board to compare the finished portrait with the model and she now held her breath as she awaited his criticism.

At last he uttered one word. 'Congratulations.'

Relief filled her. 'You're really pleased with it?'

'I'm delighted.'

Estelle left the chair to view herself on canvas and there was a silence while they waited for her comment. This is where the rot sets in, Kay thought, feeling sure that complaints were about to emerge, but to her surprise Estelle's eyes glowed with satisfaction as she looked first at the portrait and then up into Rolf's face.

'Do I really look as—as lovely as that?' she asked doubtfully.

'Yes.' His reply was abrupt.

'You're sure Kay hasn't flattered me just a little?'

'Not at all. I consider she's been very honest.'

A flush of pleasure spread over Estelle's face. 'Where shall you hang it? In your lounge or—or perhaps in your bedroom?' she added with a naïve show of shyness.

'Its hanging-place has not yet been decided,' he told her coolly. 'However, the paint is still wet, and until it dries completely I'd be grateful if it could remain here.' He glanced at Kay. 'That'll be OK with you?'

She nodded. 'Yes, of course.'

He went on, 'There's also the question of a suitable frame to be found, and your signature must be put on the portrait.' He paused as Ivy came into the room.

The older woman's grey eyes widened as they rested on the finished portrait, then she exclaimed, 'Oh, isn't that good. But then I knew it would be, because it seems to have gone well from the start. Kay dear, I've always said you should do more portraiture. When we live in Napier I think you should specialise in it. I'm sure it would pay you better than those little gannet paintings.'

The silence that followed her words was broken by Estelle. 'Are you actually saying you've decided to move at last?'

Ivy uttered a deep sigh as her glance moved from Estelle to Rolf. 'I'm afraid the writing seems to be on the wall.'

Estelle laughed happily. 'Don't you mean on the canvas?'

Ivy sighed again. 'Well, it does appear to be inevitable.'

Rolf placed a sympathetic arm about the thin shoulders that had suddenly drooped. 'Arnold having said so?' he asked drily.

Ivy ignored the question. Instead she straightened herself and said with forced brightness, 'Let's have a sherry to celebrate the finishing of the portrait. Rolf, will you do the honours for me?'

'Of course.' He moved to the cabinet and poured the drinks, and as he handed a glass to Kay he said, 'You've definitely caught her expression.'

'I'm glad you think so,' she returned in a low voice. 'I was afraid you might consider it to be a little sulky.'

'Oh, no, it's sexy, rather than sulky.'

'No wonder you're pleased with it,' she murmured, sipping the sherry which did nothing to lift her spirits or prevent the knife from twisting within her. Where would that lovely face hang? In his lounge—or in his bedroom as Estelle had suggested? Her attention was then caught as the latter spoke to Ivy.

'Naturally, Mother is longing to see it. Oh, I almost forgot, she asked me to tell you to keep next Saturday evening free. As you know, she's having a party and would like you and Kay to come.'

'That's very kind of her,' Ivy returned with dignity. 'Perhaps she could phone and offer the invitation herself.'

'But I'm inviting you now,' Estelle retorted.

'It's your mother's party, and I don't like second-hand invitations,' Ivy said calmly.

Estelle became impatient. 'Oh, it may be Mother's birthday, but it will be as much my party as hers. Isn't that so, Rolf?' She sent him an arch smile, her head tilted to one side.

He shrugged. 'Only if you steal the limelight from her.'

Estelle's smile grew wider. 'Well, that's always possible.' She drained her sherry, then placed the glass on the table. 'Now I must go home because Mother has invited guests for lunch. Rolf dear, you won't forget we're to swim at three o'clock? I've checked the tide this time. It will have turned, but Mother's guests will prevent me from coming any earlier.'

He frowned. 'I dare say it'll be OK if it has only just turned.'

Estelle spoke graciously to Kay. 'You may come with us if you wish, even if two people make company while three make a crowd.'

'Thank you, how very kind.' Kay found difficulty in keeping the sarcasm from her voice. It was easy to guess that Estelle wished to swim without her company, and she wondered if this preference also applied to Rolf, therefore she put him to the test by saying, 'Perhaps I should stay home and clean my brushes and palette.'

He spoke sharply, his words lifting her spirits. 'Rubbish. You'll swim with us.' He then turned to Ivy. 'What about you, Ivy? We'd like you to come swimming with us.'

She shook her head. 'That's nice of you, but no, thank you. I haven't been swimming since——' She faltered and fell silent.

'Since Arnold died?' Rolf prompted gently.

'That's right. We always swam together.' She hesitated, then appeared to make a decision. 'Perhaps I'll go in before the end of the summer.'

* * *

Rolf spent the early part of the afternoon at his drawing-board, but when three o'clock chimed without any sign of Estelle he sent impatient glances at his watch.

'She'll be here soon,' Kay consoled him, secretly irritated by his apparent anxiety to see Estelle arrive.

'I'm thinking of the tide,' he pointed out abruptly.

The redhead put in an appearance at last, again wearing her bikini, and as they made their way across the shingle beach she danced ahead of them before dropping her cape and kicking off her sandals prior to entering the surf. 'Hurry up,' she called. 'The water is almost lukewarm.'

Rolf followed her and together they splashed about in the waves.

Kay stood watching them for several moments then pulled on her bright yellow bathing-cap before stepping out of her sandals and wading into the water. She felt *de trop* and longed to return to the house, but feared that to do so would not only make her look childish, but would also betray her jealousy.

And there was no doubt about the intensity with which it gnawed at the depths of her soul, filling her with a desperation that vibrated through her body with the virulence of an overwhelming pain.

Turning away from the pair in the water, she then became conscious of the firm drag round her legs as the outgoing tide revealed its strength by causing her feet to sink into the loose shingle of the gravel-covered bottom. However, she decided it wasn't severe enough to worry her, nor did she feel inclined to leave the water before at least getting wet, therefore she waded in up to her waist.

For a short time she floated on her back, swam a few strokes or bobbed in the surf near the other two until Estelle's monopolising of Rolf's attention annoyed her to such an extent that she swam away from them. Jealousy continued to burn with the force of a raging furnace, and only vaguely did she hear the call of his voice.

'Don't go out too far.'

She stopped swimming and stood up to let him see she was still little more than waist-deep, then, as she turned away from him, she saw the large wave that was almost upon her. It rose above her head in an overhanging white-edged curl, and she dived into it, expecting to shoot through to the other side.

But instead of breaking the wave continued to curl downwards, sweeping her into the green gloom of its undertow and dragging her along the seabed. She kicked and struggled frantically, fighting to reach the surface, but lacked sufficient strength to escape the grip of the powerful undercurrent below the waves. While she felt herself being swept on and on her lungs reached the stage of bursting-point.

Panic siezed her, sending her heart to her throat and causing the blood to pound in her head. A fear of drowning gripped her, and her mind became a chaotic jumble wherein the only vision of any clarity seemed to be Rolf's face. Was it to be her last earthly sight before she lost consciousness, before her heart stopped beating?

Suddenly she knew she loved him, knew without a shadow of doubt that for her he would always be the only man in the world. But now it was all too late, and in any case he wasn't hers to love because there was Estelle who everyone would consider had a prior claim. If only she had time to fight for him—time to fight—time—time——

The thought galvanised her into a frenzy of mad kicking which sent her to the edge of the undertow and into the upper waves. Miraculously she shot to the surface where she gasped in great gulps of air, filling her bursting lungs which were now aching from an intense soreness, and as the sun shone on her face she became

aware of her thumping heart and an overpowering
dizziness. She also found she was unable to move
because her strength had been spent, and when she tried
to turn on her back she began to sink.

It was Rolf's arms that prevented her from going to
the bottom again, his voice shaking with anxiety that
enabled her to believe she was not about to drown.

'Hell's teeth, you gave me one devil of a fright. I
thought you'd never come up.'

'Undertow,' she murmured drowsily.

'Don't talk. I'll get you back. We're a fair distance
out.'

He swam on his back, dragging her along while
holding her head clear of the water. Progress was slow,
and she was conscious only of the firm grip of his hands
and an occasional slap of water against her face.
Although it seemed to be ages before they reached the
shore she eventually felt herself being lifted and then
carried to the shingle where she lay trembling and
weeping from shock.

Lying on her stomach, her face against the hard
stones, she knew that Rolf knelt beside her, but
although he murmured urgently in her ear she was
unable to understand his words because of her own
overpowering distress. And then the pressure of his
hands on her back caused her to vomit sea-water, the
action helping to clear her head.

'Good girl, spit it right out,' Rolf approved.

'Ugh, how *revolting*.' The exclamation of disgust
came from Estelle.

'Shut up, Stell,' Rolf snarled.

'She's putting on an act,' Estelle sneered. 'Can't you
see she just wants your attention, and she's getting it
nicely.'

'You're wrong. I watched her dive into that big wave
but she didn't come out. It was fortunate I saw her
yellow cap come up, because she'd been swept out for

about thirty yards or more.' His attention returned to Kay. 'How do you feel?' he asked in her ear, his voice surprisingly gentle.

She was unable to reply, because her body was again being shaken by sobs while ridding itself of more sea-water.

'Have a good howl,' he advised. 'Get it out of your system.'

At last the weeping subsided, enabling her to whisper huskily, 'I feel so tired, I just want to go to sleep, here in the sun.'

'Like hell you will. I'll carry you home.'

Estelle snapped angrily, 'What a load of rubbish. Of course she can walk. Anyone would think she *needed* to be carried.'

His voice became hard. 'Is it that you *can't* or that you *won't* see that much for yourself?'

'What I *can* see is that she's making a fool of you.'

Rolf gritted, 'I can't understand you, Stell. You've changed.'

She became defensive. 'Changed? What do you mean?'

'You're not the Stell I used to know.'

'I haven't changed. I'm still me, same as ever.'

'Perhaps I didn't see you clearly in those childhood days. I used to think you were full of good fun, but now I find you're just full of bitchiness.'

The voice that reached Kay's ears held desperation. 'Rolf, dear, can't you see I'm *frustrated*? You pay so much attention to *her*.'

'I can see you're completely lacking in sympathy for one who is suffering the shock of being almost drowned,' he gritted.

Perhaps his words caused Estelle to realise her attitude was unwise because her voice lost its previous scathing tone as she said, 'Do you honestly think that—that Kay almost drowned?'

'For Pete's sake, I don't *think*, I *know*. Now do me a favour, Estelle. Pick up your cape and take yourself home.' His tone was abrupt with impatience.

'But you'll—you'll come and see me soon, perhaps this evening? Just to let me know how she is, of course?'

'OK.'

Kay listened to their exchange in a haze of drowsiness. She felt herself being lifted from the roughness of the gravel, then became aware of the strength of Rolf's arms as they cradled her against him. She heard his feet crunch over the stones while carrying her towards home, and when they reached Hope House Ivy's shriek of alarm pierced her weariness.

Vaguely she knew she was conveyed up the stairs to her bedroom, and that Ivy rubbed her hair with a towel before slipping a nightgown over her head. And there was a short period when she imagined that Rolf sat beside the bed, but after that she knew nothing because she fell asleep.

CHAPTER NINE

KAY slept for the remainder of the afternoon and through the night, but if anyone had promised her that memory of the ordeal would evaporate by morning she would have been disappointed, because it was still with her when she woke, hovering in the back of her mind like a dark spectre. Nor had her weariness completely disappeared.

When she looked through the window the sight of the expanse across the bay, grey-green beneath a cloudy sky, served only to remind her of the murky green depths below the surface of the water. It caused her to shiver and she vowed she would never go swimming again.

At last she forced herself to shower and dress, and when she went downstairs she found Rolf in the studio engrossed at his drawing-board. The sight of his lean strength gave her a feeling of security and caused her pulses to quicken. At the same time she was filled with an overwhelming gratitude that sent her towards him.

'Thank you for saving my life,' she said in a low voice.

He turned to look at her, then said lightly, 'You can thank your yellow bathing-cap, which enabled me to see where you were. You should keep it in a place of honour on the mantelpiece.'

She saw no humour in the remark. 'It's easy for you to be flippant. I'm afraid the incident doesn't affect me in quite the same way.'

His arms reached to draw her against him, and holding her close to his chest his voice came from above her head. 'Poor little girl—you'll get over it, although it'll take ages for you to feel like swimming again.'

She shook her head. 'I'll never go in again. I've already decided on that.' A shudder passed through her body, causing an instinctive pressing of her cheek against his shoulder.

His arms tightened about her. 'I know you've had one hell of a fright, but we'll go swimming again, I promise.'

'And no doubt with Estelle in attendance.' Her voice rang with resentment as she recalled Estelle's words while she had been lying on the stony beach.

'Not necessarily,' he soothed her. 'We went swimming together before, if you care to remember. Just two people bobbing about in the waves.'

'How could I forget?' she murmured, thrilling to the feel of his arms, yet warning herself he was merely showing sympathy, because he made no attempt to kiss her. Yes, sympathy, that was all this little display of affection amounted to, she realised.

And then Ivy's voice came in calm matter-of-fact tones from behind her. 'Ah, there she is. Bring her out to the kitchen, Rolf. I'd be grateful if you'd stand over her while she eats a good plate of porridge.'

Kay turned to peep at Ivy, expecting to find surprise on the older woman's face, but instead it remained completely expressionless. Didn't Ivy realise that Rolf was holding her in his arms? Did she imagine this to be a normal state of affairs?

Ivy went on placidly. 'Food is what she needs. It was understandable for her to miss dinner last night but this morning is different.'

A feeling of exasperation gripped Kay. She pushed herself away from Rolf's arms then exclaimed crossly, 'You're both treating me as though I'm a child.'

He grinned at her. 'Then prove you're an adult by eating your porridge. It shouldn't be too difficult with all that raw sugar and rich creamy milk. Nor have I dragged you from the depths only to see you fade away, so be a good girl and eat up.'

Despite herself Kay smiled as he followed her to the kitchen. Was it possible his feelings for her were deeper than she realised?

Estelle arrived later in the morning, ostensibly to enquire about Kay's reaction to her ordeal of the previous day, but in reality to see Rolf. This fact became obvious when, taking Kay aside in the lounge, she whispered somewhat pointedly, 'Yesterday I came to talk to Rolf privately.'

'Oh, yes, about your engagement.'

'You'll recall I had very little opportunity to do so, therefore I intend to speak to him today, and I mean *alone*.' The last words were snapped imperiously.

'You're telling me to keep out of the room?'

'That's right.'

'Very well. He's in the studio now. I'll give you ten minutes and then it'll be time for morning coffee.' She turned blindly and went towards the kitchen, where she found Ivy spooning a fluffy pikelet mixture into the frying pan.

'Did I hear Estelle arrive?' Ivy asked.

Kay nodded, then swallowed hard before she said, 'Yes, she's in the studio with Rolf. I've promised to give her ten minutes for a—a private discussion.'

'Really?' Ivy paused to send her a sharp glance before carefully placing another spoonful of batter in the pan. 'Why do I suspect something has upset you?'

'She's come to tell him her mother wishes their engagement to be announced at the party.' The unsteadiness in Kay's voice betrayed her misery.

Ivy put the bowl of batter on the bench and began to laugh.

Kay looked at her reproachfully. 'I see nothing funny in the situation.'

'Don't you?' Mirth caused Ivy's hand to shake while

turning the pikelets that had begun to bubble.

'I can't bear to think of them becoming engaged,' Kay almost choked, tears springing to her eyes.

'That's because you're in love with him,' said Ivy gently. 'You don't have to hide it from me, my dear. I've known it for quite some time, even if you yourself haven't realised it.'

Kay was unable to speak while the tears rolled down her cheeks. She snatched at a handkerchief and dabbed at them furiously, then blew her nose.

'You needn't worry, there'll be no engagement,' Ivy assured her calmly.

'How—how can you be so positive?' Kay asked between sniffs.

'Common sense tells me,' declared Ivy flatly. 'Have you forgotten the advice given to all young men? When choosing a wife, take a good look at the mother.'

'I—I think he's quite fond of Mrs Lexington-Barron. She was kind to him when he was young, and he hasn't forgotten.'

'Hmm, well, maybe. But that's only because he's a very nice person. It doesn't prevent him from knowing she's overbearing and bossy. And the same applies to Estelle, who is growing more like her mother every day.'

'You're only trying to comfort me, but frankly I'm not convinced.'

Ivy removed the last of the pikelets from the pan, then began to butter the ones that were suitably cold. Kay placed the coffee-mugs on the tray, and both women remained busy with their own thoughts until Ivy spoke.

'There's another point that strikes me with force,' Ivy declared. 'I truly believe that Rolf has enough sense to realise that Estelle is not the woman he should be marrying. He needs someone less concerned with her own demands, someone sweet and gentle like you.'

'*Me*? Sweet and gentle? Huh, at the moment I'm

raving mad. I'm all churned up inside.'

'Then simmer down and we'll take the coffee in. I think Estelle has had long enough to convey her mother's commands.' The last words were accompanied by more suppressed giggles from Ivy.

Kay lifted the tray and followed her towards the studio, and as they approached the door apprehension gripped her. Was she about to be confronted by a triumphant and radiantly happy Estelle standing close to an equally happy Rolf? The thought made her afraid to enter the room.

However, her fears were unfounded, and while she searched for exultation in both faces, neither betrayed emotion of any sort. In fact, nothing seemed to have happened, and her spirits rose while she noticed that Rolf, completely nonchalant, continued to be busily engaged at his drawing-board.

Yet she had to know, she had to be sure, therefore she carried the tray across the room to Estelle. 'Well?' she asked quietly. 'Is it settled?'

Estelle took a mug from the tray then sent an enigmatic smile across the rim. 'Of course it's settled. What else did you expect?'

Kay turned away to offer coffee to Rolf. Her spirits had plummeted, and, while she sensed he did not appear to be as joyous as a man whose engagement was about to be announced in the near future, she also realised he was not one to toss his emotions around for all to see, therefore he would be unlikely to display any reaction at all.

Her misery did not allow her thoughts to proceed beyond this reasoning, and a short time later she felt only relief when Estelle placed her coffee-mug on the tray and said she must leave. Kay then looked at Rolf, expecting him to see Estelle to the door, but he made no move to leave his board.

Possibly it was this lack of attention that caused

Estelle to send a pointed glance at Kay and say coolly,
'I'm going home because Rolf wishes to work
undisturbed. I trust you'll allow him to do so.'

'I'm not in the habit of disturbing Rolf while he's
working,' Kay retorted, feeling thoroughly irritated.
'You may rest assured he'll have the studio to himself.'

'My day is being arranged for me?' Rolf drawled.

'You said there were details to be finished,' Estelle
reminded him. She then thanked Ivy for the coffee and
moved towards the door, where she paused to speak to
Rolf again. 'I'll see you on Wednesday.'

He frowned, searching his mind. 'Wednesday?'

She betrayed impatience. 'Yes, you said you'd be
busy until then. Don't tell me you've forgotten that
we're to make a—a most important purchase on that
day. We're to have lunch after we've been to that large
jeweller's shop in the centre of town.'

The last words hit Kay with force. Jeweller's shop?
Of course, they'd be buying the ring. She became
conscious of the dull ache within her breast becoming
more pronounced.

Estelle said, 'I feel quite excited—I'm just longing for
Saturday to come.'

Ivy looked at her thoughtfully, 'I can't say that you
appear to be excited. I mean, not really bubbling
inside.'

Estelle sent her a condescending glance. 'Oh, well,
one must not show one's true feelings, must one? It's
simply *not done*.'

Ivy then saw her to the door while Kay put the
remaining empty coffee mugs on the tray. She longed to
ask Rolf for details of the situation between Estelle and
himself, but pride kept her silent. There was no need to
betray the fact that she was even remotely interested,
she decided. And she also feared that if he did admit to
his pending engagement she would make a fool of
herself. In her present state of emotional instability she

would be sure to break down and weep. And then he would know at once that she loved him.

Nor did her despondency disappear during the afternoon when she watched him packing his drawing-board and easel into the Porsche. He had completed the work he had come to do. The plans for the transportable houses lay on large rectangles of paper that had been rolled and neatly tied with pink tape. And now it was time for his departure.

He said goodbye to Ivy by giving her a hug that lifted her off the ground while she clung to him lovingly. And then he merely brushed Kay's cheeks with his lips.

She longed to fling her arms about him, but held herself under rigid control while her heart wept.

Ivy said, 'Don't forget, you're to stay here during the party weekend. It'll be much easier than driving home to Napier, especially if you're full of champagne.'

He smiled at her. 'Thank you, I haven't forgotten.'

Surprise caused Kay's eyes to widen. This was the first she had heard of the arrangement, and it was difficult to keep the ring of gladness from her voice as she said, 'You'll be staying here? Of course we'll be delighted to have you, but won't Mrs Lexington-Barron and Estelle expect you to stay with them? After all, you'll have just become——' The words faltered on her lips and she fell silent. Then, to her extreme annoyance, her eyes filled.

He looked at her with concern. 'Do I see tears?' The words came gently.

She brushed them away, blinking rapidly. 'It's—it's just reaction from yesterday. I—I'm still in a state of—of feeling not quite myself.'

'I see. For one mad moment I thought that perhaps those tears might be because——'

Her heart leapt. 'Yes? What did you think?'

'Well, nothing of importance. Possibly I was mistaken.'

'Please tell me,' she implored.

He shook his head. 'I doubt that it would interest you.'

Frustrated, she watched him get into the Porsche and drive away. Although she told herself to follow Ivy inside the house, she remained glued to the spot until the car had become a red blur which disappeared round the corner.

The following week was a miserable one for Kay, filling her with foreboding every time she thought of the coming Saturday evening, and making her feel that the end of her world was at hand. She missed Rolf far more than she dreamed possible, and even the knowledge that he would be with them at the weekend did little to lift her spirits.

By the time Wednesday morning came Ivy was looking at her with concern. 'My dear, you're not eating enough, and you're very pale.'

'Please don't worry about me, I'll be OK.'

'But I do worry about you. In three days you've lost weight and you're dark round the eyes. You must snap out of this depression.'

Kay was amused. 'Huh, hark at who's talking.'

Ivy was unable to ignore the insinuation. 'Yes, I know you're pointing your finger at me, but my situation was different. Arnold and I were together, whereas in your case, well, he's not yet engaged to Estelle, and until he is you'd be wise to keep out of that deep ditch of despondency. I know all about that dark place.'

Kay laughed. 'It's good to hear you spouting wisdom.'

'And high time too, I suppose. Naturally, it's easy to be wise when making a present of advice to somebody else.'

'Speaking of presents, we must find a gift for Mrs Lexington-Barron because it is her birthday. What does one give to a person who no doubt has everything?' Kay asked.

Ivy became thoughtful until at last she said, 'I'm unable to think beyond an indoor plant.'

'An indoor *hanging* plant,' Kay agreed. 'You give her the plant and I'll give her a macramé hanger for it. Let's go to town this morning and get it off our minds.'

'Haven't you a few gannet paintings ready for the gift shop?'

'Yes—to be honest I'd forgotten about them.'

'So much on your mind?' Ivy teased.

'It's possible.' Kay's colour deepened slightly as she went to the studio to sort through her finished work.

Most of it consisted of small oils ready to be framed, while a few watercolours had been surrounded by mounts and then protected by a transparent film. She packed them into a flat cardboard box, and an hour later she was driving the Mini towards Napier.

As they drew near to the Parade, Ivy said, 'We'll go to the plant shop first and get that job settled. Then we'll deliver your paintings. The gift shop is near the restaurant, and by that time we'll be more than ready for lunch.'

The hanging plant was found, a delicate pale green fern with drooping fronds that caught their attention as soon as they entered the shop. A hanger on display was chosen, and they then made their way to the gift shop where the owner examined the paintings with interest.

'Thank heavens you've brought more gannets,' she exclaimed. 'Would you believe I've sold every one of your paintings? Of course it's the time of year when so many people go to the Cape to see the birds. Ah, now I like this one that includes the peep of the cliffs. I'll keep this one for myself.'

Ivy smiled at Kay as they left the shop. 'There now, that should make you feel better. Most satisfactory, I call it.'

'More satisfactory than Estelle's portrait?'

'That's different. That's what I'd call a triumph. Now would you please forget about that girl and lead me to a cup of tea?'

They entered the nearby restaurant where they decided upon sandwiches and asparagus rolls, plus the extra treat of a large cream-filled chocolate éclair. Then, as Kay carried the tray towards an unoccupied table, the sight of two people sitting in a corner of the room caused her to draw a sharp breath.

'Did you say to forget about that girl?' she hissed at Ivy.

'I can see them,' Ivy snapped, her mouth tightening. 'But if you recall, she did arrange to meet him on Wednesday.'

'I remember, but I didn't expect to run into them.'

The unexpected sight of Rolf and Estelle had brought back the inner ache with full force. Their heads almost together, they appeared to be examining the contents of a small box which lay on the table between them. Its size suggested jewellery, and Kay's suspicions were sent leaping towards an engagement ring. Well, it was all part of the ordeal she must face at the weekend, and she began to wonder if she could bear to attend the party.

Ivy looked at her shrewdly. 'You're worrying needlessly,' she declared, almost as if reading Kay's thoughts.

'What do you mean?'

'If you think they're looking at a ring you're mistaken. The box is the wrong shape. It's too flat. I can see that much even from this distance. Besides, if it had been a ring it'd be flashing from her finger right now.'

The truth of Ivy's words swept Kay with relief, causing her to laugh weakly. 'Ivy, you're such a comfort, you're just the dearest pet.'

'It takes one to know one,' the older woman retorted

drily. 'Now control yourself, because Rolf is coming this way.'

Kay refused to turn her head. 'And Estelle? Is she coming with him?' The question came anxiously.

'No, she's left the restaurant. It's possible she has to return to the boutique to allow an assistant to go to lunch.'

When Rolf reached their table Kay was able to greet him with a calm smile. Her heart contracted as she looked at him, noticing that his business suit gave him an air of sophistication yet did nothing to conceal the virile form beneath the dark grey material.

He looked from one to the other, although his eyes lingered upon Kay. 'I didn't know you were coming to town today.'

Ivy explained casually. 'Kay had to take some more paintings to the gift shop, the last lot being all sold. And we had shopping to do.'

Rolf's eyes remained on Kay. 'You look pale. What's the matter? Are you not feeling well?'

'I'm perfectly well, thank you.' She looked down at the table, finding difficulty in meeting his eyes.

Ivy declared, 'I think she's lost weight.'

'Rubbish.' Kay spoke sharply. 'I'm the same as ever.'

Rolf's eyes narrowed as they regarded her intently. 'Are you worrying about something, Kay? If you are, I'd like to help.'

She continued to stare at the table while shaking her head wordlessly. Help? Dear heaven, he was the only one who *could* help.

He said quietly, 'Perhaps we could talk about it at the weekend.'

'A good idea,' said Ivy briskly. 'At what time may we expect you?'

'Not until late on Saturday afternoon. During the day I must visit a building-site out in the country.' He told them about a large residence being planned for a wealthy farmer whose property consisted of several thousand acres.

Ivy said, 'It sounds very grand.'

Rolf looked at Kay. 'Would you like to step into such a home?'

She shook her head. 'No, thank you. Not for one moment would I swap Hope House for it.' The words had come with more force than she had intended, and to lighten the remark she added, 'Not that I'll be given the opportunity, of course.'

He grinned. 'Who knows what opportunities are at hand?'

Her brows rose. 'What does that remark mean?'

'It means your efforts on Estelle's portrait might bring results. You've signed it, I hope.'

'Yes, but I still don't know what you mean.'

'I agree with Ivy. You shouldn't be wasting your talent on gannets. I intend to have your portraiture put on display. It might result in commissions. That's what I mean by opportunity.'

'I see. Thank you, you're very kind—but how and where?'

'You'll learn soon enough,' he said gravely, then left them and strode away from the restaurant, becoming lost among the crowds walking along the footpath.

'He's a good friend,' declared Ivy.

'Who wants only friendship?' returned Kay.

The remainder of the week dragged while Kay made an effort to keep busy with her brushes, but although there were times when Ivy found her gazing unseeingly through the window, the older woman made no comment. Instead, she went upstairs to talk to Arnold.

Fortunately, the concentration necessary for successful painting proved to be a therapy which played its part in soothing the turmoil of Kay's mind. It controlled her emotions by pushing Rolf's face into the background where it sat as a shadowy blur.

However, there was nothing shadowy about the vitality of the man when he arrived late on Saturday afternoon, and Kay, who had been listening for the sound of the Porsche, felt herself go hot as her heart began to thump. Nevertheless she hung back, remaining in the studio while Ivy greeted him.

The next instant he was staring at her from the doorway, his brilliant blue eyes flashing over every detail of her appearance. The sight of him sent more colour to her cheeks, and she felt tongue-tied until the object in his hand enabled her to speak in a casual manner.

'Oh, you've had a frame made.'

'Yes. I measured carefully, so it should fit. Do you like it?'

She nodded, examining the ornate gilded frame which was a suitable width for the portrait, the gold matching various shades in the dress. 'It's an expensive one,' she remarked, knowing only too well the cost of framing.

'So what?' he grinned. 'The work deserves it.'

'And the subject as well, I suppose?' she asked, an inner twist causing a definite pain.

He ignored the question by opening a paper bag he had carried with the frame. 'I think I've brought everything necessary.'

She then watched as the portrait was slipped into its surround, secured with small nails and the back neatened with brown self-adhesive tape. Metal screw-eyes were put in place, a cord attached, and the portrait was ready for hanging.

He then spoke to Ivy who had stood watching from the doorway. 'There now, how does it look? Do you think she'll like it?'

'She's mad if she doesn't,' Ivy retorted crisply. 'Estelle should be delighted with it.'

'And her mother? Will she also like it?' Without

waiting for a reply he went on lightly, 'I've a roll of gift-wrap and some ribbon in the car. I'll fetch it and perhaps you could make one of those fancy bows that go on parcels.'

During his absence Kay stared at Ivy in mute indignation until she said in a voice that shook with misery, '*Gift-wrap. Ribbon*. It's an engagement present for Estelle. Do you realise I've been putting my best effort into his *engagement* present?'

'That's not unusual, dear, because your best effort goes into all your work,' Ivy consoled.

Kay's voice quavered. 'The thought of this party gives me the horrors. I'm not going to it,' she declared with sudden decision.

Ivy looked startled. 'But you must, dear. You must make the effort.'

'I shall not be there. I'll have a thumping headache instead.'

'That will be lowering the flag. It'll tell him you can't bear to hear the announcement of his engagement to Estelle. If I were you I'd keep the flag flying.'

Kay looked at her thoughtfully. 'OK, I suppose you're right.'

'Of course I'm right. And you'll wear your best dress.'

Rolf's return prevented further discussion, and when he handed the ribbon to Kay she began to twist and fold its golden length into a multi-looped satin-like ball. Her fingers shook slightly, and although Rolf watched her effort he made no comment before turning to enclose the portrait in the brightly coloured gift-wrap.

Nor did he have much to say during the evening meal, and as Ivy served his dessert she said teasingly, 'You're very silent for a man who is about to become engaged. At least, that is what we've been given to understand.'

He gave a short laugh. 'Who says that's about to happen?'

Kay spoke quietly, her voice full of accusation. 'When Estelle was here last Sunday she assured me it was all settled.'

He scowled. 'Do you honestly believe I can be so easily manipulated?'

Kay tried to control her tongue, but despite herself the words slipped from her. 'I recall she arranged with you to visit the—the jeweller's shop.'

'That's right. I helped her to choose a birthday gift for her mother. She decided upon a brooch.' His voice became grim. 'What did you imagine we were buying?'

Ivy said artlessly, 'We saw you examining a purchase in the restaurant. Kay felt sure it was a ring. She was rather upset.'

The words brought a gasp of horror from Kay as she flashed a glare of fury across the table. 'Ivy, *what are you saying?*'

Ivy remained calm. 'Well, you *did* think it was a ring, and I know that you *were* upset.'

'I was *not* upset, I couldn't care less if he—if he throws himself away on Estelle.' A sob rose to her throat as she sprang to her feet and fled from the room.

Rolf called to her. 'Kay, just a minute, I want to talk to you.'

She raced up the stairs, ignoring the sound of his voice that called to her again, then flung herself into her room and slammed the door. Turning the key, she stood leaning against the panelling, her hand pressed to her mouth while the tears fell.

His fist hammered on the other side. 'Open the door. You were right, I did buy a ring, but it was later.'

'I don't want to hear about it,' she shouted furiously.

'I would like to show it to you.'

'Just take it away. I'll see it soon enough, when it's being flashed round the room,' she added bitterly.

His voice came angrily. 'Kay, open the door, there's something I must say.'

'I don't want to hear it.' She knew exactly what he wanted to say—words to the effect that they'd always be *good friends*, even if he married Estelle. Well, she didn't want to hear it.

'It's important.'

'It can wait. You can tell me later.'

'Then you will come to the party? You've no intention of locking yourself in there for the night?'

It was the only thing she longed to do, but pride came to the rescue. Her chin raised she retorted with dignity, 'Of course I'm coming. I wouldn't miss it for worlds. Now if you don't mind I intend to get ready. I must shower and fix my hair.'

'OK, I'll see you later.'

She delayed going downstairs for as long as possible and by the time she entered the lounge splashes of cold water on her face had removed all trace of tears. The steam from the shower had sent her roller-set hair into a halo of dark auburn waves, and the white strapless dress with its tiered flounces gave her an air of sophistication. Keep the flag flying, Ivy had said. OK, she would do just that.

However, she felt slightly numb from steeling herself into facing whatever ordeal the evening was about to present, and this, she feared, must surely be the announcement of Estelle's engagement to Rolf. Hadn't he admitted to having bought the ring?

Rolf stood up as she entered the room. He regarded her intently, then said in a husky voice, 'Kay, you really are quite beautiful.'

'Thank you.' She suspected he was merely being kind because she had made such a fool of herself.

However, Ivy's comment was more to the point. 'I *said* you've lost weight. Your eyes are enormous.'

'They're like large velvety pansies,' Rolf added as his eyes raked her features.

Kay smiled faintly. 'Thank you for the compliments.'

She then examined Ivy, who wore a royal blue dress patterned with threads of silver. The sight of it surprised her, causing her to say thoughtlessly, 'That's a lovely dress, Ivy. I haven't seen you in it before now.' She paused, annoyed with herself for having made such a stupid remark. Was she so wrapped up in herself that she couldn't remember that Ivy hadn't been living a social life?

Ivy smiled faintly. 'I haven't worn it since I went out with Arnold. He gave it to me. He always liked me to look nice.'

Arnold. Of course. She might have known. She then flicked a glance at Rolf, hoping he realised it was quite an occasion for Ivy to be going out for an evening's social entertainment. 'Shall we go?' she asked, picking up the gift-wrapped plant and moving towards the door.

Rolf carried the portrait while Ivy bore the macramé hanger for the plant. The air of the summer evening was still and warm as they walked the short distance along the road where numerous cars were already parked. The Barron house was ablaze with lights, and as they approached the front door the sound of music, voices and laughter floated from within.

Kay hesitated at the bottom of the steps leading up to the porch. She was filled with a strong desire to go home, but almost as though sensing her reluctance to enter the house Rolf took her arm and drew her forward. There was nobody in the hall to greet them, therefore they entered and placed the plant and hanger on the table among other parcels, while Rolf stood the portrait against the wall. He then led them into the lounge.

CHAPTER TEN

THE room was crowded with guests, and as Rolf stood among them his air of distinction set him apart from the rest.

Estelle saw him from across the room, the sight of him bringing an exclamation of relief as she hastened to greet him. 'Rolf, I thought you'd never get here. I suppose *other people* kept you late.' The accusing glance she swept over Kay and Ivy spoke for itself.

He gave her a look of appraisal, then said sincerely, 'You're very attractive tonight. I'm glad you're wearing that dress.'

She glowed beneath his words of admiration and Kay had to remind herself that he merely spoke the truth because Estelle definitely looked attractive. She was wearing the green and gold dress that Kay knew so well, her extra make-up causing her to look quite exotic.

'Come and meet everybody,' said Estelle, making an attempt to drag him further into the room.

But Rolf stood firmly. 'Do you intend to leave Ivy and Kay standing alone on the fringe of the crowd?'

'They can mingle,' Estelle declared airily.

'How about a few introductions?' he hinted.

'Oh, Mother will attend to it, but I want you to meet some special people before—*you know what.*'

He frowned. 'How can I possibly know *what*?'

A light laugh escaped her. 'Rolf darling, why must you continue to tease me? You know perfectly well that Mother expects——'

His face darkened. 'Estelle, I think we need to talk. Can we go somewhere private?'

'Of course. I'm sure Ivy and Kay will excuse us.' The

171

smile she sent Kay was a mixture of pity and triumph.

As Kay watched them leave the room she felt as if she had been turned to stone. Her voice low, she said to Ivy, 'When they come back she'll be wearing a ring.'

'I'll believe that when I see it,' snorted Ivy.

'He has got a ring, you know——'

Further conversation was impossible at that moment because Mrs Lexington-Barron joined them, her duty as hostess foremost in mind. She appeared to be in a state of suppressed excitement, almost as though expecting a momentous event to occur, the anticipation causing her flushed face to match the swathes of cerise nylon encasing her ample bosom.

'Ah, there you are,' she boomed above the surrounding chatter. 'So *very* pleased you could come. How nice you look, Ivy, and you too, my dear. Quite charming.' She flicked a brief glance over Kay then looked about the room. 'Hasn't Rolf come with you?'

'Yes, he's here.' Kay sent her a steady look then steeled herself to add, 'He and Estelle have gone somewhere to talk privately.'

Mrs Lexington-Barron beamed. 'They have? Well now, that's most exciting. No doubt you understand what it's all about?'

'I—I think so,' replied Kay faintly. 'I can only hope they'll both be very happy.'

She smiled bravely, knowing this to be a sincere wish, and telling herself that eventually she herself would escape from the grip of these icy fingers of depression. The heart of the matter concerned Rolf's happiness, and if he had decided it lay with Estelle, well, so be it.

Mrs Lexington-Barron took Ivy's arm and said, 'Come, you must meet people. Now these are my very dear friends, Colonel and Mrs Cranmore-Jones . . .'

Glasses filled with champagne were offered to them, hot and cold savouries were presented by uniformed hired caterers. Kay found herself chatting to numerous people whose names she was unable to remember, and within a short time the pale liquid she sipped made her feel less tense.

Ivy, also, appeared to have relaxed. At first she had clung nervously to Kay's side, but soon she had drifted towards people she had met with Arnold. They seemed to revive old times for her and Kay soon realised that Ivy was beginning to enjoy herself.

But where were Rolf and Estelle? Why were they taking so long to return to the room? The minutes passed while, despite the glass in her hand, Kay's depression began to wrap itself about her like a dark cloud. After all, it shouldn't take long to place a ring on a girl's finger, so what were they doing? Of course, they were in each other's arms. Where else would they be? she asked herself.

And then she saw them enter the room and was immediately swept by a sense of shock as her acute observation told her that here was no newly engaged couple. Estelle's features were a pale mask, while Rolf's face was grim. And even as she met the redhead's eyes Estelle sent her a look of undisguised hatred.

However, their lack of bubbling joy did not appear to register with Mrs Lexington-Barron who, primed by her own bubbles from a bottle, did not pause to look closely at the pair. Her voice echoed across the room as she exclaimed, 'Ah, my *dears*, there you are at last. Rolf—my *dearest* Rolf—I believe you have a surprise for me.'

Her words brought a sudden hush of interest from the guests, and above the silence his answer came clearly. 'Yes, I have something for you. I'll fetch it.'

'Fetch it?' His words had left her nonplussed.

He disappeared into the hall, then returned with the portrait. 'My birthday present to you,' he smiled, handing it to her.

Taken aback, she could only gape at the rectangular

parcel.

'I bet it's a mirror,' somebody guessed.

'Or an outsize in trays,' another voice guessed.

'Go on, open it. We're all agog with curiosity,' others pleaded.

Mrs Lexington-Barron's fingers were unsteady as they tore away the gift-wrap and revealed the painting. Her jaw sagged slightly as she stared at it, then her eyes went to Rolf. '*This is for me?*'

'That's right.'

'But I thought—I thought it was being done for yourself.'

'It was easier to allow certain people to think so. It kept the secret of its being my present for you,' he admitted drily. 'Tell me honestly, do you like it?'

'Oh yes, I'm delighted with it. Thank you, Rolf. Would you please hang it for me?'

The picture above the mantelpiece was removed while the portrait was hung in its place. There were exclamations of amazement as Estelle looked down upon the guests.

'Gosh, that's excellent,' declared an admiring voice.

'It's the image of her,' echoed another.'

'It's an oil—say, just look at the dress.'

'Who painted it? What's that name in the corner?'

Rolf answered the last question. 'The name is Kay Carlson. She is here with us this evening.' He crossed the room to stand beside Kay then added, 'Let me introduce you to the artist.'

Kay felt herself go hot as the praises floated about her. She hadn't expected this situation to arise and the universal acclaim made her feel embarrassed. People began to make enquiries about sittings and it was in a daze that she heard Rolf's voice in her ear.

'You're on your way,' he muttered. 'You'll now become the fashion with people in high places. Dare I say I told you so?'

She looked at him gratefully, her cheeks flushed. 'I had no idea the portrait was for Estelle's mother.'

'You were too obsessed by other thoughts to guess?'

'Yes, I—I suppose so.'

'And this evening you were quite positive it was an engagement present. I could read it in your face.'

'Well, everything seemed to point that way.'

'Everything? Please be more explicit.'

'Surely your request for the portrait was enough to tell me that a closer relationship with Estelle was in the air.'

'You jumped to your conclusions on that alone?'

'Not exactly. There were also your activities during the fortnight you spent with us. They certainly made me think.'

He frowned. 'Now you've got me really puzzled. Activities such as what?'

'I'm talking about your careful examination of Hope House, to say nothing of the installation of the dishwasher. It was all enough to suggest you were about to move in on a more permanent basis.'

'Surely a man may examine his own property without being expected to announce his engagement.'

'Yes, I suppose so.' Kay fell silent, suddenly aware of Mrs Lexington-Barron's presence. During her conversation with Rolf, Estelle and her mother had stood a short distance away, and although Kay had noticed the glances that had darted in her direction she had thought nothing of them until she realised the older woman had edged close enough to overhear Rolf's last words.

The face she turned to him was wreathed with smiles. 'Rolf dear, did I hear mention of an engagement?'

Estelle, who had followed her, drew a sharp breath. 'Please leave it, Mother, you're probably mistaken.'

'No dear, I shall not leave it. Nor am I mistaken. I definitely heard Rolf speak of his engagement and I want to know——'

'Mother, will you please *shut up*!' hissed Estelle furiously.

Mrs Lexington-Barron's eyes sent a flash of green from Rolf to Estelle, her voice rising as she demanded in a forced bantering tone, 'What is this mystery? Are you two naughty children keeping something from me?'

Estelle became desperate. 'Mother, please keep your voice down. You're telling the world.'

This was a fact. The guests, sensing tension between mother and daughter, had fallen silent and were even crowding closer to listen. However, the warning was ignored as the raised tones continued to reach every ear in the room.

'Have you two become engaged without letting me know? I insist upon knowing the truth, and then we can turn this function into an engagement party. So tell me honestly, Rolf, have you marriage on your mind?'

There was a breathless hush as everyone awaited his reply. When it came it made Kay feel faint.

'Yes,' he drawled casually. 'Kay and I are to be married.'

Mrs Lexington-Barron's jaw sagged as she gawped at him. '*Kay*? Are you saying you intend to marry—this girl?'

Estelle snapped at her coldly, 'I warned you to shut up, Mother.'

Kay was unable to believe the words floating about her head. She turned wide eyes towards Rolf and found him smiling down at her. 'That is so, isn't it darling?' she heard him say blandly.

She nodded dumbly, knowing he expected her to play her part. His arm had been twisted and this was his only way out from under the net suddenly thrown about his shoulders. And although the fact that he was simply using her was abundantly clear, she was unable to do other than return his smile before receiving felicitations from all sides.

Perhaps the warmest came from Ivy, whose close hug made no secret of her delight, but in whose ear Kay whispered, 'Be warned, it's all a sham.'

Ivy was startled. 'What do you mean?'

'It's only pretend. I'll explain later.'

'I don't believe it,' Ivy retorted above the surrounding chatter. 'It's not something about which Rolf would make pretence.' Yet her eyes were troubled as she watched him receiving congratulations from nearby guests.

'Wouldn't he? Huh, just you wait and see. It was his only course and he took it. I'll be thanked politely when we get home, and then there'll be nothing to show apart from the bitter hatred of Estelle and her mother.'

A glance at the latter showed Mrs Lexington-Barron to be taking the blow on the chin with all the dignity she could muster. Being under the gaze of so many people from high places, she was at a distinct disadvantage. Her heightened colour indicated that her blood-pressure had soared, but she was unable to let fly with all the fury that raged within her ample bosom, or even to point in dramatic silence towards the door. Therefore she took the only course possible by declaring that glasses must be filled to toast the happy couple, and when Estelle disappeared from the room nobody seemed to notice her absence.

For Kay the rest of the evening passed like a hazy dream, although she warned herself to keep her feet on the ground, and against reading too much into Rolf's attentions and the endearments which were now quite openly showered upon her. At the same time she gloried in the pressure of his hand on hers, and advised herself to laugh, drink and be merry, even if tomorrow she died. And that would be when he came clean and admitted he had used her.

The evening ended at last, and although she was still

in a high daze when they reached home she knew that now was the time to come down to earth. Rolf would offer an explanation at any moment and she would be expected to understand and to accept his gratitude.

But perhaps it was Ivy's presence that caused him to avoid the subject because when they entered the kitchen by the back door he merely said, 'Would anyone like a cup of Milo, or perhaps Horlicks?'

Ivy sent him an arch glance. 'No, thank you, it's long past my bedtime. I'm going straight upstairs. Besides, I'm sure you and Kay have much to talk about.'

'It can wait,' he said nonchalantly, taking milk from the fridge, then turned to Kay with a smile. 'Milo or Horlicks for you?'

She looked at him steadily, a sense of anticlimax creeping over her. He could saddle her with a bogus engagement and then offer her Milo instead of an excuse for his behaviour. No doubt he expected the hot drink to soothe the avalanche of anger he expected to erupt at any moment.

But even as her mind searched for stinging words she was engulfed by an overpowering weariness that made her long for bed, therefore she said, 'No Milo, thank you, and you may offer your apologies in the morning.'

'Apologies?' The word came sharply.

'That's right. I must say you picked a fine time to propose.'

She turned abruptly and left the room, and as she dragged her feet up the stairs angry thoughts flitted through her head. There now, that'll give him something to think about. It'll tell him I've taken the whole affair seriously. He'll begin to worry about being really engaged and at least I'll have been engaged for one night. It'll be the shortest engagement on record.

The thoughts, mingling with a deep hurt that he should do this to her, continued to swim in her head while she undressed and removed her make-up. Then, before climbing between the sheets, a sudden impulse caused her to lock the door. If Rolf imagined he could come striding into her room he would meet a barrier.

Nor had she been in bed for more than a short time before there was a tap on the door, then the handle turned while Rolf's voice called to her. 'Kay, are you still awake?'

'Go away, I'm almost asleep.'

'I think we should talk.'

'Can't it wait till the morning? I'm very tired.'

'I feel I owe you an explanation.'

'Huh, you can say that again. Go to bed.'

'Kay, please, I want to talk to you.'

'To break off our *engagement*, I suppose.' The words were accompanied by a ring of bitterness over which she had no control. Then as the tears began to trickle down her cheeks a feeling of emotional exhaustion came over her. No matter how hard she tried she was unable to hate him, and in some strange way her anger evaporated while her love for him surged up to bring sympathy, understanding and forgiveness to the fore.

His voice came from beyond the closed door. 'Kay, please.'

'It's all right, I understand you were in a hole. I was glad to help you scramble out of that sticky situation.' The fact that it mocked her own feelings for him was beside the point.

'What the devil are you talking about?'

'I'm trying to tell you there's no need for you to lose sleep through a night of worry.'

'*Worry*? What do you mean?'

She spoke calmly. 'Can't you see that you made a rash jump from the frying pan into the fire? You tied yourself to me instead of to Estelle. Or hadn't you realised that?'

'Of course I realised it. So what?'

'Well, you spoke before witnesses, so I suppose it

could be quite binding, but there's no need for you to fear repercussions. I have no intention of holding you to any such commitment.'

His answer came in the form of a fist banging on the panel while his voice came angrily. 'Kay, do you want me to break down this door?'

'Well, it is your door.'

'I tried to talk to you before we left for the party, remember?'

'I do. Was it with this plan in mind?'

'No, it was not.'

'Oh?' Her curiosity was aroused. 'So what was it about?'

'I do not intend to shout the details through this door.'

'*I should think not.*' Ivy's irritated voice came to Kay's ears. 'May I be told what causes this argument in the small hours of the morning? If not, would you mind allowing a body to get some sleep?' The next instant her door was shut with more force than necessary.

There was a moment's silence before Rolf rasped at Kay, 'We'll continue this discussion in the morning.' The words were followed by the slam of his door.

When morning came Kay woke early and was immediately conscious of a depressing weight on her mind. And as the events of the previous evening crowded back she knew she was anything but anxious to continue the discussion that would break off the engagement which really did not exist.

Gazing at the ceiling, she asked herself questions. If it didn't exist, why should she be concerned? Because she longed for it to exist, of course—and during the coming discussion she feared she might betray this to Rolf. She knew her eyes were expressive, and she was afraid her love for him might shine from their depths. Would she even dare to look at him?

Obviously, her easiest course would be to avoid the

discussion. But how was this possible when he was in the house and unlikely to leave before the afternoon? The answer to that problem lay in her own movements, she decided.

If she slipped out quietly and did not come home until late afternoon he might leave before she returned to the house. With luck he would get the message. He would realise she had no wish for discussion of any description, and the question of the engagement would blow away on the breeze.

The decision made she left her bed hastily and was soon in the kitchen. The silence of the house suggested that Ivy and Rolf still slept soundly after their late night; nevertheless she moved as quietly as possible, rapidly eating a breakfast of cornflakes, fruit and milk, followed by tea and toast.

She then made cheese and tomato sandwiches, filled a flask with boiling water, and a small bottle with milk. Teabags completed what she intended to be her lunch. They were placed in an old satchel that had once belonged to Arnold, and to them she added her watercolour pencils and a sketching-pad.

In the studio she remembered to put a large-brimmed hat on her head, and she was about to snatch up her painting-stool when she changed her mind. Instead she would sit on the ground, so she collected a small rug from the cupboard beneath the stairs.

She left the house without a sound, her intention being to make her way along the shore towards Cape Kidnappers where she might get sketches of gannets. But she had forgotten about the tide, and, as she had no intention of being caught against the high bare cliffs when it was full, she made her way in the opposite direction.

Walking along this particular beach was never easy, but she trudged on and on until she was out of sight of the houses. She then made her way towards the upper reaches where vegetation edged the stony shore, and, spreading the rug between large clumps of marram grass, she settled down to think.

Lying on her back, she stared up at fluffy puffs of white cloud floating against the blue and, as she pondered whether or not she had been wise to dodge the issue by running away, weariness began to steal over her. She shook herself, trying to pull herself together with thoughts of becoming busy with her pencils, but despite her efforts her eyes closed and she slept.

About an hour later Rolf's voice pierced her slumber, causing her to open her eyes and blink up at the tall figure standing above her.

His voice held a hint of amusement as he drawled, 'Your own bed was so uncomfortable you sought another? I must say you've walked far enough to find it.'

She stared at him wordlessly, taking in the length of well-shaped legs, bare beneath the hems of his shorts. Then she sat up and spoke defiantly. 'I decided to do some early-morning sketching.' The pad and watercolour pencils were dragged from the satchel by way of proof.

He looked about him. 'What subject did you have in mind? I see nothing of particular interest.'

'Oh, well, there's the sea. It takes practice to get the curl of the waves breaking on the beach—and a seabird might land close at hand,' she explained without looking at him.

'All of which can be found close to home,' he pointed out.

She ignored this obvious truth by asking, 'Are you out for a morning walk?'

'No. I came to find you.'

'You did? To continue last night's discussion, I suppose.'

'That's right. Last night's discussion which you

appear to be so determined to avoid. How long did you intend waiting here before making sure I'd left? Until tomorrow morning maybe?'

She flushed beneath the sting of his irony, then asked, 'How did you know where to find me?'

He sat on the rug beside her. 'I saw you make your way in this direction.'

'Oh, so you weren't asleep.'

'No. Nature's call drove me out of bed. You had left your door open, which enabled me to see that your bed was empty. I realised you must be downstairs, but by the time I got there you were crossing the road. I then watched from an upstairs window while you headed this way. You looked like a lonely tramp.'

'Thank you.'

'After that I gave Ivy breakfast in bed, then came to find you—to continue the discussion.'

She remained silent, waiting for him to go on.

'Last night before we left for the party I said I wanted to talk to you. I intended admitting I love you.'

The words were spoken in a flat, emotionless tone, causing her to wonder if she had heard correctly. Slowly, she turned to look at him, her voice coming as a mere whisper. 'I—I didn't know——'

'No. But that's because you wouldn't listen.'

'How could I possibly realise when—when I was so sure you were about to become engaged to Estelle?'

'It was never Estelle. From the moment we met I've been drawn towards you. Why do you think I brought that work project to be done at Te Awanga?'

'I presumed—to be near Estelle——'

'You were wrong. It was because I knew I had to see more of you. Nor could I believe my luck when Ivy invited me to stay at Hope House. Surely you realise the job could have been done in my own flat, despite my excuses about noise.'

'Again I thought——'

'It was because of Estelle? Again you were way off base.'

'But you were checking the house so carefully. How could I think other than that you intended moving in with her? I mean, after your marriage, of course.'

He gave a short laugh. 'Needless to say, that idea had also become stuck in her mother's mind. Mrs Lexington-Barron has the single purpose of a missile on its way to its target, and the announcement of Estelle's engagement was to have been the highlight of her party.'

'How can you be so sure about that?'

'Because Estelle had been quite frank about it. She never could keep a secret, as I think I've already told you. You'll recall that when we arrived I took her aside. I explained that marriage between us was impossible because I was in love with you.'

'Poor Estelle.' Kay's voice was a low murmur of sympathy.

'I expected her to have a word in her mother's ear, but before she could do so the dear soul had made a bid to bring me to heel, or matters to a head, as it were.'

'It must have been a bombshell for her.'

'Under the circumstances I think she behaved very well. There was no fit of the vapours while she collapsed in a chair and kicked her legs in the air. And now only one question remains.'

She looked at him shyly. 'Yes? And that is——?'

'Is there any chance that you could possibly——?'

'Love you? Rolf, I've been so afraid you'd see it written all over my face.'

'Then tell me, my darling,' he muttered huskily, his arms snatching her to him. 'Let me hear you say it.'

'I love you, Rolf,' she whispered against his lips.

'Dearest, I'm hungry to know—when did you first realise?'

'Oh, that's very clear. It was when I was in the

undertow. I think it was the fear of never seeing you again that gave me strength to kick my way out.'

'Thank heaven you did. Strangely, that's when I realised for sure that I loved you. When you didn't come to the surface I experienced real panic. I knew I couldn't live the rest of my life without you.' He bent and kissed her lips with a gentleness that suggested he was keeping a tight rein upon himself.

'Tell me more,' she pleaded, savouring the odour of his aftershave. 'When did you begin to suspect that I—that I might mean more than a casual acquaintance to you? I'm well aware that it wasn't love at first sight.'

'How do you know, oh, wise one?'

'Because when we met you were raving mad with me. I'd stopped the Mini on the Parade without a signal, remember?'

'Indeed I remember.' He grinned ruefully. 'OK, so I'll now have the grace to admit I was travelling too close behind you. Does that satisfy you, my dearest little petticoat driver?'

'Only partly, because I want to hear more. I mean about when you discovered——'

'You're asking when I discovered I had to fight against it?'

'Did you—have to fight?'

'Yes.' He frowned in a thoughtful manner. 'I suppose it began with admiration for your ability to use paint. And as it grew I assured myself it was mere infatuation, stirred by a pair of pansy-brown eyes.'

She laughed. 'Sir, you do have a way with words.'

'I mean them, especially when I say I need you, my beloved. I want you beside me for the rest of our lives.'

She gloried in the sound of his deep voice and in the feel of his arms holding her against him. His lips on hers, his hands lovingly caressing her body made her ache with longing to be closer, and as he slid further down to lie stretched beside her on the rug she saw the glow of love in his eyes.

As her arms wound about his neck her senses rose in quick response while a tremor of desire caused her to arch towards him. The involuntary movement dragged a small moan from him, and, crushing her against his body, he made no secret of his arousal.

His voice came in a low, husky murmur. 'Darling, you know I want you—and I know that you want me.'

She nodded shyly. 'Yes, I know, but please—can we wait——'

'Yes, but not for too long. When can we be married?'

'As soon as possible. I don't want a large wedding, but my mother will insist that it takes place from our home in Wellington.'

'Waiting for even the shortest time will drive me up the wall.' He changed his position, but as he gathered her to him again something hard in the breast pocket of his shirt pressed against her ribs. A sharp corner of the object caused sufficient pain to force a small gasp from her.

He drew back, looking at her with concern. 'Darling, what is it?'

'Something in your shirt pocket. What is it?'

'Oh, *that*—I'd forgotten about it. Last night, if you recall, I wanted to show you a ring, but you wouldn't look at it.'

'How could I bear to look at it? I was sure it was for Estelle.'

'It was for you, if you would accept it.' He unbuttoned his shirt pocket and drew forth a small box.

She stared at it, wide-eyed. 'You've brought it along the beach?'

'Of course. It's part of the discussion that was to be continued. Care to look at it now?' The question came nonchalantly, and without waiting for her to reply he flicked the lid open.

Kay was bereft of words as she found herself dazzled

by the morning sun's rays falling on a brilliant solitaire. 'It's—it's quite magnificent,' she breathed wonderingly.

Rolf slipped it on her ring finger, then took her in his arms again. His lips found hers, kissing her in the way she had dreamed of being kissed. She felt the thump of his heart against her own and knew instinctively that he had never kissed Estelle in this manner—had never told Estelle that he loved her.

Her uninhibited response equalled the passion building within him until suddenly the pulsing grip in his strong fingers told her he was calling for control. A sigh escaping him, his mouth left hers to trail across her brow before finding its way to nibble gently at her cheek, and from there it traced a line along her jaw.

She felt his lips caress her throat, and she knew his fingers had unfastened the buttons on her blouse. And as his cheek pressed against the soft roundness of her bared breast a surge of tenderness caused her to hold his head even closer. Then, as her fingers stroked his heated brow and ran through his thick hair, the solitaire glittered among the dark strands.

Again her eyes widened in disbelief at the sight of it, and she realised it heralded a new beginning in her life. From now on everything would be different, and her thoughts went to Ivy. What did Rolf have in mind about Ivy?

Tentatively she said, 'Ivy will be pleased about us.'

'Ivy already knows.' The statement came casually. 'We had a short chat over her breakfast tray. I've assured her she'll be free to live in Hope House for as long as she wishes, provided she agrees to share it with us.'

'She's unlikely to object to our presence, especially yours, because when you're near Arnold has returned.'

'She mentioned something about that, but I pointed out that the time would come when she'd have more than Arnold on her mind. He'd be replaced.'

Kay was puzzled. 'Replaced?'

'By our babies.'

The mere thought made Kay's heart leap. She laughed happily, then asked, 'What did she say?'

'She declared she'd vacate the master bedroom at once.' He looked at her flushed face. 'Darling, you do want a family?'

She nodded. 'Of course.'

He went on, 'I also intend to retain the flat on the Parade. It'll serve as our city residence when we attend social functions in town, and as a studio for your portraiture, if you feel inclined to continue in that line.'

She felt a surge of ambition. 'Yes, I'd love to try.'

'It would be more central for people who haven't the time to travel to Te Awanga for sittings. Businessmen, for instance.'

'You mean people in high places,' she laughed.

'You can believe it. Remarks I overheard last night indicated that at least three women with daughters intend to keep up with Mrs Lexington-Barron. I'd say you've finished with little paintings for tourists. A new era is about to begin for you.'

'I have you to thank for it, my beloved,' she said softly.

'I've merely set your feet on a track in line with your ability. The rest is up to you.'

Her eyes glowed at the thought of the busy life ahead of her, a life filled by the man she loved and work which gave her the greatest satisfaction.

Rolf's voice came fiercely. 'But you just remember, I shall not tolerate less of your attention being given to me than to some old boy with bags under his eyes. However, I'll try to be impartial towards your sitters, and not jealous at all.'

'Thank you. I'll choose them carefully. Nothing young and dashing!'

He kissed her again. 'Darling, I love you so much it's

like a sharp pain that can't be rubbed.'

'And I love you, my dearest. No portrait in the world will ever come between us, I promise. In any case, I'd have Ivy to contend with. She'd be down on me like a ton of bricks.'

He laughed. 'Dear Ivy—I can understand Arnold loving her. She said that tonight she'd be thanking her lucky stars.'

Kay's arms tightened about him, the joy that filled her seeming to overflow. She gazed beyond the top of his head, still resting against her breast, to where a dark speck soared with outstretched wings. It hovered above the sun-sprinkled ocean before diving towards the depths with incredible speed.

'The stars?' she murmured softly. 'Yes, I'll also thank my lucky stars, but my real gratitude goes to the gannets. It was the gannets that brought us together—if you remember.'

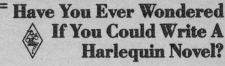

Have You Ever Wondered If You Could Write A Harlequin Novel?

Here's great news—Harlequin is offering a series of cassette tapes to help you do just that. Written by Harlequin editors, these tapes give practical advice on how to make your characters—and your story—come alive. There's a tape for each contemporary romance series Harlequin publishes.

Mail order only

All sales final

THE LOVES OF A CENTURY...

Join American Romance in a nostalgic look back at the Twentieth Century—at the lives and loves of American men and women from the turn-of-the-century to the dawn of the year 2000.

Journey through the decades from the dance halls of the 1900s to the discos of the seventies ... from Glenn Miller to the Beatles ... from Valentino to Newman ... from corset to miniskirt ... from beau to Significant Other.

Relive the moments ... recapture the memories.

Look now for the CENTURY OF AMERICAN ROMANCE series in Harlequin American Romance. In one of the four American Romance titles appearing each month, for the next twelve months, we'll take you back to a decade of the Twentieth Century, where you'll relive the years and rekindle the romance of days gone by.

Don't miss a day of the CENTURY OF AMERICAN ROMANCE.

The women...the men...the passions...
the memories....